MW01382965

BOOK 2

ROCK *Fuck* CLUB

A POST SEASON ONE NOVELLA

MICHELLE MANKIN

Sign up for my bimonthly Black Cat Records' newsletter. There's a giveaway each month and a chance to win an autographed paperback and swag.

Link to subscribe: http://eepurl.com/Lvgzf

ABOUT THE AUTHOR

Michelle Mankin is the *New York Times* bestselling author of the Black Cat Records series of novels.

Rock Stars & Romance. Love & Lyrical Ever Afters.

Love Evolution, Love Revolution, and Love Resolution are a BRUTAL STRENGTH centered trilogy, combining the plot underpinnings of Shakespeare with the drama, excitement, and indisputable sexiness of the rock 'n roll industry.

Things take a bit of an edgier, once upon a time turn with the TEMPEST series. These pierced, tatted, and troubled Seattle rockers are young and on the cusp of making it big, but with serious obstacles to overcome that may prevent them from ever getting there.

Rock stars, myths, and legends collide with paranormal romance in a totally mesmerizing way in the MAGIC series.

Catch the perfect wave with irresistible surfers in the ROCK STARS, SURF AND SECOND CHANCES series.

Romance and self-discovery, the FINDING ME series is a Tempest spin off with a more experienced but familiar cast of characters.

Exploring the sexual double standards for women, the ROCK F*CK CLUB series is a what-if the groupies called the shots instead of the rock stars.

When Michelle is not prowling the streets of her Texas town listening to her rock or NOLA funk music much too loud, she is putting her daydreams down on paper or traveling the world with her family and friends, sometimes for real, and sometimes just for pretend.

OTHER BOOKS BY MICHELLE MANKIN

BRUTAL STRENGTH series:
Love Evolution
Love Revolution
Love Resolution
Love Rock'ollection

TEMPEST series (also available in audio):
Irresistible Refrain
Enticing Interlude
Captivating Bridge
Relentless Rhythm
Tempest Raging
Tempting Tempo
Scandalous Beat

The MAGIC series
(also available in audio):
Strange Magic
Dream Magic
Twisted Magic

ROCK STARS, SURF AND SECOND CHANCES series
(also available in audio):
Outside
Riptide
Oceanside
High Tide
Island Side

FINDING ME series (also available in audio):
Find Me
Remember Me
Keep Me

ROCK F*CK CLUB series
(also available in audio):
Rock F*ck Club #1
Rock F*ck Club #2: A Postseason One Novella
Rock F*ck Club #3

CONNECT WITH MICHELLE MANKIN

on Facebook: https://www.facebook.com/pages/Author-Michelle-Mankin/233503403414065
On Twitter: https://twitter.com/MichelleMankin
On her website: http://www.michellemankin.com/
On Instagram: https://instagram.com/michellemankin/

Sign up for the Black Cat Records newsletter where I give away an autographed paperback and swag every month: http://eepurl.com/Lvgzf

Rock F*ck Club #2: A Postseason One Novella

10 cities. 10 famous rock stars f*cked.

Raven Winters has chosen the one rock star she wants to keep. She has completed filming for the Rock F*ck Club. Her season of the reality show is about to debut on the World Media Organization channel. Her once very private sex life is about to become public.

Can her life ever return to normal?

Does she want it to?

And what about the next season of RFC?

Who will be the next star?

Who will be f*cking whom?

ROCK
CLUB

CHAPTER
one

"SHHH," I WHISPERED INTO MY PHONE. "Not so loud. He's sleeping." I tucked my cell between my shoulder and ear and slid as quietly as I could from the middle bunk. The sleeping area on the bus was dimly lit, the thick curtains on all the other compartments drawn. The road noise hummed steadily as we rolled along to the next venue. "Give me two seconds." Snagging my robe from the hook, I hurriedly belted it on, my naked body awash in goosebumps beneath the thin layer of silk.

Yeah, I slept in the nude now. Lucky preferred easy access that I was more than willing to provide since I usually got lucky whenever he had it.

"I'm heading to the front lounge now." I winced as I skated down the narrow aisle between the bunks. The air conditioning was set too low. The floor felt like an ice rink beneath my bare feet.

"Alright. I'm here," I announced breathlessly. "What's going on?" Three a.m. phone calls that bolt you out of a deep sleep and start with the words, 'I need to talk to you right now. It's an emergency' were never good. "Are you ok?"

"I'm ok *now*. Now that I finally have you on the phone," my best friend Marsha West declared with dramatic flair. "I just needed to hear your voice."

"At this time of the morning?" My racing heart slowed. I narrowed my eyes. "How many drinks have you had, Mars."

"I dunno. More than a couple. I stopped counting. That's Joey's job."

"Joey, the bartender back home?"

"Yeah, the home you *used* to have. I don't know why you keep your old apartment anymore. You never use it. It's a waste of money."

"I keep it because it's where I live when I'm there and where I keep all my stuff while I'm out here on the road."

"You weren't on the road when you had that long break in La-La Land," she grumbled. Man, she was irritable. "You never came to visit me once. Not even one single time."

"What you call a break included a whole lot of work, Mars. In addition to all the pre-publicity interviews and stuff to promote Rock Fuck Club, Lucky and the guys had to put the finishing touches on their new album."

"So you were busy. Fine. Whatever. I'll give you that. But it's been weeks since then, Raven. Weeks since I've heard from you. So what's your excuse for not even picking up the phone to say hi?"

"The Dragons are on tour. My boyfriend..." I paused, the relational identifier still made my heart flutter, "is the lead singer."

"I know who Lucky Spencer is, and I know what you've been doing with him. Showing him your tits and shagging." She mimicked his British accent. Poorly.

"I'm sorry, Mars. Things have been hectic."

"Not that hectic. Not too hectic for a simple phone call. Not for a true friend. For a *best* friend. One who only knows where you are because I can see it on the Dragon's website."

"I…"

"Once upon a time," she cut me off. "I was your wing woman. Back in those not that long ago days, I seem to recall my cell working just fine. On that tour bus. Yours too, now that I recollect." Her Texas twang got more pronounced when she was worked up. "I certainly didn't have any difficulty on my end just now getting ahold of you."

"I know the cell service works," I huffed. "It's a time issue. Since 'She's the One" became a number one hit, the Dragons are headlining their own shows. The band and I, we're up all night, every night. We do a show, steal a couple of hours of sleep while the bus rolls along through the night. Then we wake up in a new city and we do the whole drill all over again. Interviews and promo slots first thing in the morning. Sound check in the afternoon. Concerts at night. I think about you all the time. I miss you all the time. But I never get a quiet, private moment to call you. Night time is the least busy, but it's been so late I haven't wanted to wake you."

"That's a lot of rambling, Raven." She sighed heavily. "You ramble when you're deflecting. Why don't you just go ahead and tell me the real reason you haven't called me?"

"Which is?"

"You don't need me anymore. You have a new best friend. One I can't compete with. One with a cock."

She might have been joking, only I knew she was not. The bus swerved. So did my stomach as I fell backward onto the leather couch behind me. An inelegant landing, my arms were strewn wide and my legs askew. I rocked back and forth sideways before the driver righted the vehicle. The bus really needed a couple of well-placed handholds.

Seat belts wouldn't be such a bad idea, either. I had hit my head once and bruised other body parts on more than one occasion. But my uneasiness right now had less to do with the hazards of bus travel and more to do with the fact that I'd hurt my best friend. Even though it had been unintentional, I'd allowed distance to develop between us. It was my fault she felt shut out and abandoned. Abandonment had been an emotional trigger for her since her mother had taken off in the middle of the night, leaving her and the rest of the family without any forwarding address or explanation. Marsha had been only fourteen at the time.

"You're my best friend, Mars. I would be lost without you. I will *always* need you. That will *never* change. I apologize for not keeping in touch. I haven't been a very good friend. It's just that Lucky and I are new, and I've never been in a relationship that's so intense, so *consuming*. Besides with everything else going on in our lives, it's stressful, too." Marsha and the Rock Fuck Club crew might not be following me around filming me anymore, but there was still tons of stuff to deal with for the show, and Lucky had his band commitments as well. Rarely did we have a moment to ourselves when a moment for ourselves was what I wanted most. "I feel like a sardine. Along with Lucky's bandmates and his sister, we're crammed in the same little tin. Lucky and I rarely have any privacy. Plus, we have responsibilities that send us in different directions most days. We never seem to have a moment of time for each other, much less for anyone else."

"Raven, I'm sorry." She suddenly didn't sound so irritable anymore. "I didn't think about how things must be for you. I was too preoccupied feeling sorry for myself and wallowing in juvenile emotions. I should've made a point to call and check up on you sooner."

"You're not clairvoyant, Mars. And your feelings are valid. I missed you. I should've at least called and let you know how things were going."

"You can tell me now."

"It might take a while."

"I've got time. Not a lot to do on my end. I paid off all my debt, thanks to you and World Media Organization. I sent out a bunch of resumes. I sit around waiting for nonexistent job offers to come in. The old groove back in the Big D minus you is pretty fuckin' boring if you wanna know the truth. So spill what's up with you."

"Boring actually sounds pretty good to me. Enviable even." I turned my head. The sleeping section remained a dark portal, but I had left the sliding door open. I got up and closed it. "Are you somewhere you can talk? I don't want you driving after you've been drinking."

"I'm inside the bar. I just left Joey's apartment." The bartender had an apartment above the bar. He and Marsha were often at odds. They had a bizarre antagonist with benefits arrangement. I didn't understand it. "I was going to call a car service to take me home, but I'll just sit down for a bit and chat with you instead." I heard the sound of wood scraping against wood. I could picture her hitching up one of her sexy dresses, shimmying onto one of the tall barstools, throwing her straight blonde hair over her slim shoulder and turning her pretty baby blue eyes my way to regard me. "Pretend you're here."

"That's actually what I was doing," I admitted feeling a sharp wistful pang.

"You putting yourself in your usual spot?"

"Yeah for sure. Right beside you on my favorite barstool by the neon Lone Star Beer sign." I tried to rub that wistful burn from my chest. "I wish I really was there with you right now."

"A couple of shots glasses. A bowl of fresh cut limes. Salt. Some Two Rows Back music playing on the jukebox."

"If only." The pang became a piercing.

"Close your eyes, honey. Use your imagination. Try harder. We'll pretend together. Take as long as you need to get there and formulate your thoughts. I'm an excellent listener."

"I know you are. I could really use your sympathetic ear."

"You've got it. You've got me. The doctor is in. Dr. West, pseudo psychologist at your service."

"Forget the shots glasses, what I need is that whole freakin' bottle of tequila."

"Then grab one. I know those Dragons. I've partied with them. Their on board bar is well stocked." She had a point. I stood and crossed to the built in kitchenette. I popped open the cabinet door above the sink. "Dammit, we're out of tequila," I complained. "We're due to stock up in Atlanta. Nothing left in the cupboard but Rocky's protein shake mix and a half bottle of Lucky juice."

"His Captain Morgan's spiced rum?"

"Yeah."

"That'll have to do."

"There's no glasses."

"Then swig it straight from the bottle, honey, just like he does."

I didn't need any further coaxing. I tipped it back and gulped a big swallow. My eyes watered as the seventy-proof elixir flooded my taste buds and set fire to my throat. I coughed, recapped the bottle and returned it to the cabinet. Warmth infused my limbs. My lips formed a bemused smile. My mouth now tasted like him. "Done," I informed her. "But Dr. West, you do know you could lose your license prescribing alcohol to your patients."

"Hey, I'm not a real doctor I only sleep with them if they're cute. I prefer rock stars when given a choice. Just like my bestie. And don't dis my methods. Some of the best therapy in the world happened right here in this bar with you and me and a bottle of Cuervo."

"The liquor might have loosened my tongue. But the rest was all you, Marsha. You and your friendship. Your willingness to listen. You. Just you."

"Oh, puh-lease. Stop being a motivational meme and tell me what's going on already."

"I don't know where to start."

"Start at the beginning. You're gonna have to bring me up to speed."

"When was the last time we talked?"

"When I called to let you know I got home safe from LA, remember? Our last meaningful conversation was probably way before that on the Thelma and Louise car ride to Monument Valley before Lucky showed up."

"That long ago?" I blew a wispy strand of black out of my eyes.

"Yeah, babe. Thus, the best friend wakeup call in the middle of the night. I've already got the general picture. You and Lucky, and your private Rock Fuck Club for two. Did I get that right?"

"Yes. Only you left out a bunch of adjectives. Life transforming. Out of this world amazing. Blazing hot."

"I'm not sure if those really qualify as adjectives, but I get the idea. He's great in bed. You two are smokin' hot together, Raven. That's the consensus on social media leading up to the debut of the series on WMO. There are some haters, sure, but for the most part everyone seems to like you two as a couple. I think that's the main reason you escaped a severe reprimand from Suzanne Smith for violating your contact."

"Ten different cities, ten different rock stars," I muttered defensively. I had given the senior VP in charge of new programming at WMO everything I had promised. "I didn't violate my contract. I delivered."

"Hmm. Maybe technically, and the way we edited the footage to feature all those hot looks and weighted glances between you and your man no one's gonna complain too much about the head count. It's all sexy TV-MA beginning to end. But you and I both know those last two supposed fucks were total bullshit. No kissing. Barely any touching. Both hookups bandmates of the man you denied having a relationship with when you signed on the dotted line."

"Yeah, you're right. I know." I sighed.

"So what is it? What's going on besides life transforming, amazing, blazing Lucky sex?"

"You'll find out for yourself soon enough."

"You coming to see me in Dallas?" Her tone brightened.

"No." I sighed again. "I have to go to New York tomorrow evening. Well, this evening," I added considering the hour. "I've been summoned to WMO headquarters. The spin we put on the last part of Rock Fuck Club. Well, Suzanne's not sold. And I'm betting it's only a matter of time before you and the rest of the film crew get a call similar to mine. Your name has certainly been bandied about and not in a positive light."

"Oh no," she whispered.

"Oh, yeah. That severe reprimand you think I avoided? Not so much. She laid into me and then some. And I'm afraid there's more of the same on the way. Only she's going to serve the next portion to me in person. I'm afraid things are about to get a whole lot worse."

CHAPTER
Two

"RAVEN," LUCKY CALLED, AND I CHANGED my position on the leather couch, turning away from the window to look at him instead. He was a much better view than the concrete freeway divider. His handsome features and glacial blue eyes shadowed by a black avalanche of bed tumbled hair, the lead singer of the Dragons wore only a pair of his silky black boxers and nothing else. No eyeliner. No silver rings. None of his rock star accessories. Just him. The guy who held my heart. "Are you aware of the time?" Slim hips, long legs, sculpted arms, every inch of his sexy six-foot-two frame moved in mesmerizing concert as he came closer.

"Yes. Sorry. I didn't mean to wake you. I know it's early."

"Apologies aren't necessary, Angel. Why couldn't you sleep?" His eyes searched mine for answers. "What's bothering you?" He reached for me, captured my hands and pulled me toward him. He placed my hands on the center of his hard chest and wrapped his strong arms around me. I tilted my head to maintain his gaze. The warmth within it and the heat of his body flowed into me. I willed my troubled thoughts away. "You've been up all night again haven't you?" His eyes narrowed disapprovingly. "Did you sleep at all?"

"A little," I hedged, but that had been prior to Marsha's call. I ducked my chin. My long hair slid forward, ribbons of ebony forming a curtain to shield me from his prying gaze.

"A little's not enough." He removed one of his hands from my lower back, curled his forefinger under my chin and gently brought my head up. Pools of empathetic aquamarine beckoned me to reveal all. "I thought I wore you out sufficiently enough to sleep soundly." He framed my face in both of his hands caressing my skin with soft soothing sweeps of his thumbs.

"You did." I shivered, recalling exactly how he had done it.

"So why..."

"Marsha called."

"In the middle of the night? Is she ok?" I had shared stories with him about how Marsha and I had courted trouble over the years. It wasn't surprising his response was similar to mine.

"Yeah, but she misses me. I miss her. I've been neglectful," I summarized.

"More like I've been monopolizing you." His thoughtful brow dipped. "And Rock Fuck Club takes up the rest of your time. But I'm sure she understands."

"She does." After she had finished going off on me, I had shared, and she had listened. Then she had advised me to level with Lucky. So level with him I did. "Suzanne Smith called." I felt his muscles stiffen beneath my hands. "A while back actually."

"A week ago?" he guessed, his brow dipping dangerously low.

"How did you know?"

"That's when you started having trouble sleeping."

"Oh. You're very observant."

"I am when it comes to you." His aquamarine eyes frosted his displeasure. "You should have told me about this when it happened."

"I know, Lucky." I touched my fingers to his lush lips before he could sound off on me like she had. "But that was when all the extra tour stops got added. Then you and Alec argued, and Sky had her meltdown." Apparently Cover Girl liquid liner from CVS was not the same as MAC cosmetics. I knew better now. So did everyone else on the bus. "The last thing I wanted to do was add to the stress."

"You only do that when you keep things from me and bottle up what's bothering you. I've been worried. How can I help you if I don't even know what's going on?"

"That's just it, though. You can't help me. Not against WMO." He didn't realize that he had a hero complex, but he did. And one of the tenets of that complex was intolerance to seeing those he cared about being bullied. Rescuer. Defender. Protector. Lucky played those roles for me and just about everyone else on board the bus. "This is my mess. I thought it was over, but I should've known better."

"You're the star of the show. The founder of a movement that's caught fire. I'm not sure it's realistic to believe it will ever be over."

"But I did my part. We filmed the last episode. The production crew disbanded. The outrage that motivated me to try to overturn the sexual double standard for women? It's not the driving force in my life anymore." My fingers flexed on his skin. I wanted to stamp the truth of the next words onto his heart. "You are."

"You're my heart, too, Raven." He peered at me through the thick fringe of his inky-black lashes before bringing my hands to his lips and brushing a soft kiss across my knuckles. My skin tingled with warmth. "Let's focus on that. On each other." He lifted his head, holding me captive with his compelling gaze. "Make that our priority. The other things in our lives will fall into line. You started out with a sincere goal for RFC to rectify something you saw as an injustice. The parts we don't like? The consequences that result from it? We just have to deal with them as they come. We've already been through the flames. They refined us, made us stronger and surer of each other and what we are. We're a team you and me. We'll get through whatever Suzanne Smith or anyone else throws at us together."

"I love you," I declared, throwing the windows of my soul wide open to let him see that he had all of me. I slipped my hands from his grip, but only to lift them so I could press my palms and my fingertips into his. I was commemorating this moment, his words, and my commitment to him. Touch and sight aligned in the way of the Navajo.

"I love you, too, Angel." Shifting closer, he lifted my hands to his neck and slid his into my hair. Tugging on the strands, he encouraged me to tip up my head as he lowered his own. Blue, blue, a vast expanse of limitless blue filled my vision as his mouth hovered a breath away from mine. I closed my eyes as he closed his. We were so finely in sync, yet I was never fully prepared for the devastating onslaught that even just a light touch from his lush lips wrought.

His kiss was gentle at first, his mouth brushing my own. But that gentleness was enough to generate a whole lot of heat when my soul was dry kindling, and he was the crackling spark. Less of the lesser me, more of the better, I reveled in the woman who emerged from those flames. His love made me powerful, and I belonged to him.

He deepened the kiss and passion transcended thought as his tongue probed the seam between our lips. He demanded access, and I gave it to him, moaning into his mouth and melting more each time his masterful tongue lashed my own.

"Lucky." I broke the connection between our mouths. My body was molten fire and wet heat. "Each time, every time," I panted, my fingers tangling in the thick strands of hair at his nape to keep him close. "I don't think it can get any better, but it does. You make me so hot."

"I want you. *Now.*" His response was guttural, and I clung to him as he trailed warm, lingering body and soul melting kisses over the round of my cheek and then down my neck while his hands glided lower and lower along the length of my spine.

"Uh-um." A masculine throat cleared. "Do you two mind?"

"Yes, we do. Bugger off," Lucky mumbled into my neck, his breath humid against my skin, his fingers digging deeper into the rounded cheeks of my ass. "Can't you see we're busy?"

"You've been 'busy' half the night already." Rolling his jade green eyes, Alec Harris, the Dragons' obsessive compulsive bassist came further into the lounge with his usual careful, precise stride. "Don't you think you should give it a rest?" He stopped a foot away from us.

"You might need a breather to recharge, old man." Lucky often teased his best friend about the fact that he was a month older. "But I don't." He stroked the back of his hand down my cheek. "Not with Raven for inspiration."

"Fine, mate. But take your *inspiration* to your bunk or the back lounge. Some of us have important shit to do." Alec was the practical one in the group. A good foil to Lucky's more fluid artistic mind most of the time, but sometimes they butted heads.

"Raven *is* important." Lucky bristled.

"Granted. Apologies." He tipped his chin. Not a single wisp of hair framing his angelically handsome face moved out of it proper place. "But we can't put off Charles Morris much longer. He wants us to select the song order for the live album."

"He'll get it when I'm good and ready."

"Timing's important, Lucky. He's just trying to capitalize on the success of 'She's the One'. He sent me three emails yesterday. You do remember that he's the bloke who signs our paychecks."

"I know exactly who he is. He's the sod who's all fine and accommodating when he wants something, but he disappears when things go balls up like what happened with JGB and Raven."

"John Got Busted is a rapper on his label. He gave you a heads up and a list of lawyers for her. What more did you expect? Raven's your girlfriend. We all love her, but she's not an official member of this band. Morris isn't all that bad. You forgetting he leant you his penthouse in LA?"

"Now there's the point. That concession didn't cost him a pence, and he got a brand new album from us ahead of schedule. I'm not forgiving and forgetting that he didn't have my girl's back when that blighter talked shit about her in the media. Charles Morris can wait to get what he wants for a change." Lucky gave his best friend a hard look. "What's got you all miffed this morning?"

"Not a what. Who." Cody Charles, the rhythm guitarist, Alec's partner, stepped into the lounge. His sandy curls were disheveled and his gunmetal grey eyes were bleary. He looked like he had just rolled out of his bunk.

"Let's not revisit this." Alec narrowed his jade hued gaze on the man he loved. "We said all there is to say last night. I didn't appreciate what you insinuated. I would never..."

"It's hardly insinuation," Cody interrupted. "You kissed someone else."

"It was a club. She was simply a waitress selling shots. It's part of the experience for her to put the test tube in her mouth and tip the contents into mine. My lips never touched hers."

"Nevertheless, you hurt my feelings." The usually carefree rhythm guitarist's grey eyes glassed up. The two men were opposites in a lot of ways. Alec was reserved in sharing emotions. Cody wore his out in the open.

"I got that."

"My sleeping in another bunk sent the message, did it?"

Alec nodded. "Come here." He crooked his finger. Cody crossed to him. "Forgive me?" Alec's voice was rumbly soft.

"Perhaps." Cody firmed his lips. Alec framed his partner's face in his hands.

"You must know it meant nothing except that it bothered you. I never meant to hurt you." Alec lowered his face and kissed Cody, deeply. Cody remained stiff for less than two seconds before he melted into Alec's strong arms. I flushed with heat just watching their hands wandering all over each other. Both were well-built, extremely sexy guys wearing tight matching boxer briefs that outlined their attributes. Hotties with hard-ons. They were always a demonstrative couple. This morning was no exception. They rarely bothered to shut curtains or close doors whenever the mood struck them. It added an interesting dimension to life on the bus.

"Bullocks!" Rocky Walsh, the Dragons' powerhouse Welsh drummer stopped short inside the threshold to the lounge. He shook his head at the bassist and the rhythm guitarist who were still going at it. "I thought we had a rule in place about this early morning PDA." Rocky looked like he had just woken up, too. His normally circa 1960's Keith Richards styled hair looked more like mahogany porcupine quills, a fact that in no way detracted from his hotness. All the guys in the band were good looking men. The fishbowl we lived inside of might be overcrowded, but the fish that swam in it with me were handsome specimens, even more so in close proximity.

The drummer casually sauntered closer to the couple. His expression not hinting at what he had in mind, he thunked Alec on the side of the head and then punched Cody in the shoulder before quickly stepping backward to get away. Both men broke apart and came at him.

"What's your problem?" Alec asked.

"Yeah, you shit!" Cody lifted his chin. His sandy ringlet curls shivered with his irritation.

"No problem." Rocky threw his hands up and turned away. "I just have a titanic headache." His half buttoned jeans riding low on his hips, he rifled through one drawer and then another. "Where's the bloody aspirin?"

"What's your headache have to do with me and Cody?" Alec wouldn't let it go.

"Everyone on this bus knows how you two are, Rocky returned. "You argue so you can make up. I don't want the bus rocking just now. I'm liable to chunder."

Ah, the explanation for why the drummer had woken sans his usual good humor.

"Aspirin's on the second shelf," I informed him. "Pepto's just behind it."

"Cheers, Raven." Rocky gave me a grateful look before he opened the fridge and took out a bottled water to swallow the pills.

"Morning all." Sky Spencer emerged from the bunk area. The last one to wake, she brushed past the hungover drummer on her way to her brother. Rocky shifted to watch while Lucky shifted to receive the kiss his sister planted on his cheek. The pretty brunette did hair, makeup and stage clothing for the band. Her sweet effusive personality was a balm to the rest of us when the stress of the road got to be too much. "Morning, Raven." She skipped to take a seat at the banquette. Her feet rarely ever dragged.

"Morning, Sky." Rocky was the first to return her general greeting.

"Morning, poppet." Alec moved closer and kissed the top of her head.

"Morning, luv." Cody slid into the seat across from her. Sky gave me an expectant look. She was ready for the breakfast I usually prepared for her. Everyone on board was present and accounted for. The morning routine was poised to begin. A typical hectic day for the band lay ahead with one major variation, my trip to New York.

"Porridge with fruit, coming up." I pasted on an efficient smile, refusing to let the stress and the thought of leaving get to me. I pressed my hands and fingertips together as I crossed to the kitchenette. Recalling Lucky's touch and remembering his words, I regained the serenity I'd had a moment earlier within his embrace. I only hoped it would last longer than our brief moment of privacy had.

CHAPTER
Three

"How many hours till Atlanta?" From her spot at the banquette, Sky frowned at the remaining fruit on her plate as if she hoped her displeasure could transform it into a big heaping bowl of chocolaty Maltesers, her favorite candy.

"Three, dearest," her brother replied without taking his eyes off of me as I slid a cup of Earl Grey toward him. He lifted it to his mouth. The steam caressed the rugged planes of his handsome face the way I wished I had time to. "Thank you, Angel." He blew across the heated surface. I tried to focus beyond the pleasurable quiver that came over me as I remembered where those lips had been on my body just minutes earlier.

"You're welcome." With everyone taken care of, I took the space he made for me on the bench beside him.

"The cantaloupe was brilliant with the porridge, Raven." Sky gave me a sheepish look. "Thanks for it, but I'm afraid I can't manage another bite." Sky was very thoughtful, always eager to please. But she was struggling with her diabetic diet and often didn't finish what I put in front of her.

"It's ok, honey," I reached across the table and squeezed her hand. "Just eat what you can." She had only recently been diagnosed, and while she understood the need to follow the strict guidelines what she really longed for was sugar.

"I get the shower first today." Rocky threw that general statement to everyone. We all remained in the front lounge that served as the communal area when we were on the road.

"Sure. Sure," Cody responded without looking away from whatever version of Mario he was playing. Flopped on one of the couches, he stared raptly at the overhead screen.

"Fine by me." Alec waved an agreeable hand in the air, his gaze glued to his iPad while he reached for the plate of carefully partitioned food I had set on the couch cushion between him and Cody. His toast was in equal fourths, and his cantaloupe wedges were all facing the same direction. It went without saying that none of the items could be touching one another on the plate. "But fold your towel afterward and put it back on the rack instead of on the floor."

The drummer rolled his eyes at Alec before glancing at the lead singer. Zero chance Rocky would follow that directive. He didn't take orders. He gave them. "Alright if I have a turn in the loo before you, Lucky?"

"Yeah, though you might want to wait until we get to the hotel in a few hours. Raven and I are."

"Right. Well, I'll take my chances now." Rocky's gaze drifted yet again to Sky. She was rearranging her fruit rather than eating it, but the drummer wasn't watching her hands. He was looking down her shirt at her exposed cleavage. The plastic casing of the water bottle he held crinkled as he crushed it in his grip. I had a pretty good idea that the rush to the shower out of the usual order —Alec (because he had to have it first in the morning before everyone else messed it up), Cody, Lucky and me, Rocky then Sky- was because the drummer needed to finish off what seeing Sky's tits had started. His morning wood had grown into a monster-sized erection. He shifted and adjusted himself quickly.

Yeah, glad I would be taking my shower at the hotel.

"Sit up straighter, luv." Lucky reached across the small table and lifted his sister's chin. She gave her brother a puzzled look but corrected her posture. Rocky jerked his gaze away from Sky. The lead singer turned his attention to Rocky, narrowing his eyes. "Have your shower, arsehole."

The drummer nodded.

Sometimes, I thought Lucky was oblivious to the undercurrents between Rocky and his sister. Other times like now I think he noticed everything and just chose to chime in when the drummer's interest had crossed some unwritten line in his mind.

Sky turned her head, keeping her gaze on Rocky until the bathroom door closed and the lock clicked. She swiveled back around, caught me watching her and blushed. She had totally been checking him out.

"Have some protein, Sky, my dearest," her brother ordered. "We have a little cushion of time at the hotel before sound check, but it's not much. I'd rather not visit the ER if you have another sugar crash because you've let yourself be distracted by certain things."

"You're right. I'm sorry." She bowed her head, more pink splashed on her cheeks. Lucky knew Sky was in love with Rocky and that his rejection of her was an open wound. Why had he called attention to it just now? Sure, they were drawn toward each other as if they were planets caught in each other's gravitational pull, but neither would act upon it. They had ample opportunity. They looked. They longed. But they never went beyond friends-only type touches.

"Sky's alright." I resisted kicking him under the table, but I wasn't going to hold my tongue when I felt that he had been too harsh. "Don't give her a hard time." The brunette lifted her head, and eyes the same striking shade as her brother's beamed her gratitude at me. "If you wanna get onto someone for messing up our schedule and causing us to be late to Atlanta blame your best friend." Alec had violated a cardinal tour edict. We had lost half a day at the previous stop in Kansas City having the lone restroom sanitized.

"Sod off, Raven. You try holding it in when you got the hangover shits."

"Oi, don't hate on my bird for pointing out the obvious. She's new to the road but even she knows the rule."

"Yeah." Sky's lips twitched in an upward direction as she entered the conversation. "It's just shit you deal with living on a bus."

"Good one, Sky." I giggled.

"Told you to go in the plastic bag, luv," Cody deadpanned, his giveaway grin awash in blue reflecting from the screen across the aisle from him. But he didn't break his concentration on the game. His controller clicked rapidly as he popped open boxes releasing one coin after another in a steady rhythm.

"Fuck the lot of you." Alec threw his iPad on the couch, stood and stomped toward the back. But I knew he wasn't really mad even though we'd been having fun at his expense. His gaze meeting mine, he paused and dipped his chin before continuing on. That was his way of letting me know he knew what I had been up to and approved. Sky's happiness was sacrosanct to all of us. Even to her brother who normally was her top defender. Ironic that it had been Lucky this morning who had crossed the un-crossable line.

"JUST GIVE ME a moment," Sky said as she exited the bathroom, a towel secured around her reed thin form.

"No problem. Alec and Cody already took off. They're gonna check us in and get our room keys." No use clamoring off the bus until we had them. "I don't mind waiting until you get dressed." I continued typing on my laptop, pretending not to notice Rocky's eyes following Sky as she headed toward the back. The bathroom had barely enough room to get your clothes off. Most mornings, after three guys, it was a total disaster: wet towels on the floor, whisker stubble all over the counter and sticky toothpaste everywhere since Cody and Rocky never capped their tubes mostly to irritate Alec. Not surprising that Sky and I preferred to get dressed elsewhere. We had a small cachet of clothes stored in the back lounge closet. We had also co-opted the fold out dressing table as our own, keeping the mirror and the counter nice and clean and off limits to the guys. The stabbin' cabin now included glamorizing.

"How many emails did you get today?" The drummer's singsong voice interrupted my musings.

"Two hundred." I lifted my gaze. Across the banquette from me Rocky had started drumming his fingers on the tabletop.

"Blimey, that's a lot."

"It's usually more." I sighed and massaged my tired hands. They were dexterous from all the years of classical training on the piano, but the motion I used on the computer keyboard was different. I needed to power through the discomfort. The next venue had an upright grand I longed to try out. I had a new composition I wanted to work on. But I had RFC emails to answer first, and I was only a quarter of the way through my inbox.

"It would be nice if you had someone to organize your agenda and sort through all that for you."

"I can see that." I flicked my gaze to the couch where Lucky sat. He was speaking quietly to the Dragons bespectacled manager. They were going over the schedule for the day. Rocky's comment wasn't out of the blue. Lucky and I had gone round and round about me approaching the WMO to ask for an assistant. But I certainly wasn't going to ask the big media conglomerate for any special favors right now with the VP in charge of my show pissed at me.

"It's gotten to be too much for you to do on your own."

"Yeah, I know." I nodded.

"It's going to get even worse once the series airs." Rocky reached across the table and covered my hand with his own and squeezed. "Denying there's an issue isn't going to make it go away, Raven."

"I realize that." I lifted a brow. That bit of wisdom could also apply to him and Sky. "I'm managing alright. I do what I have to do to get by. I'm sure you can understand." The lack of secretarial help was just one of many issues cutting into my time with Lucky. His priority was always my well-being and vice versa. But how we went about achieving those objectives sometimes differed. It was hard enough to carve out space in our schedules for each other. I'd rather the time we did have as a couple not be wasted on arguments. What I needed was more hours in the day, not another person to keep track of. Not another fish in our crowded bowl.

"Hey." Lucky touched my arm. I hadn't realized his meeting was over. I had missed watching him saunter over, and that was sad because his sexy stride was something I didn't like to miss. "Manager's gone. Got a whole list of stuff to do today." He frowned at Rocky's hand on my own.

"You're such a possessive prick." The drummer rolled his eyes but removed his hand.

"You ready to go inside the hotel?" Lucky asked.

"Sure, but I promised Sky I would wait for her." I lowered the lid on my laptop. It clicked as it closed. I wasn't near finished with my task, but RFC could wait. It would have to wait. No way was I squandering hotel room time with Lucky.

"I'll take care of Sky," Rocky offered in a solemn tone. "I'll make certain she gets in the hotel safely." When it came to Sky, he was always serious.

"Ok." I scooted out into the aisle, stood and stretched to loosen my muscles.

"Keep her away from the press." Lucky ordered Rocky inclining his head to the row of windows opposite us. "There's already a shit ton of them with the fans lined up outside."

"Done."

Shouts, catcalls, appreciative whistles, and several piercing screams suddenly reverberated through the walls.

"Show us your abs, Cody!"

"Alec, lift up your shirt. Show us what you've got!"

"I love you!"

"Sign my tits!"

We all three exchanged glances. Resigned ones. Some version of this voracious insanity had accompanied every stop lately, evidence of how rapidly the band's popularity was escalating.

"How big's the crowd this time?" My eyes were wide as I stared at Lucky. We'd had several close calls already, and I'd almost taken a header onto the pavement when an overenthusiastic group of well-wishers had surrounded us at the last venue.

"At least a hundred," he replied. "Maybe more." His brows dipped in concern. "The car park is filled with people. You'll need to stick close." His expression serious, he pulled me into him, threw his arm around my shoulder and tucked me safely into his side. But as he steered us down the center aisle, I knew it would likely take more than his strength to keep me there. Even with roadies acting as security at the last stop, I had almost gotten hurt, and the crowd in Kansas City had been half the size of this one.

As we turned the corner and started down the stairs, the screaming outside the bus rose in volume. Cody had probably taken off his shirt again. He had a ripped torso, and he liked the appreciation from the fans. He flirted and played along with them. Male or female, they universally loved him. I think he overdid it a bit sometimes, overcompensating for Alec's discomfort in the limelight, but whatever his motivation the result was good for the band, and good for the rest of us. Happy Cody fans, distracted Cody fans meant the rest of us could usually slip by with less notice.

"Has local law enforcement been notified?" I asked as we stopped on the stair opposite the driver's seat.

"Yeah, our manager rang them, like he did at the last stop, but you know how long it usually takes for them to arrive."

"Yeah, but it might be safer to wait." I glanced up at him, my pulse racing as more screaming rattled the door in front of us.

"Normally I would, Angel." His features tightened. "But it's my last chance to spend some time alone with you before your flight." Lucky pointed with his chin over my shoulder. "I'm taking precautions. I borrowed some things from the crew." He reached past me. His rock-solid body brushed mine as he reached for something on the driver's seat behind me. His mandarin and rum scent along with his warmth spiked my heartrate. I suddenly was every bit as eager as Lucky to get off the bus. "Put these on." He had two black support staff shirts and two black ball caps in his hand. He offered me one set and kept the other for himself. He hung the hats on the endcap of the handrail.

"Alright." I nodded. We were going incognito into the crowd. I quickly drew one of the shirts on while he did the same. He was quicker and helped me with mine. He smoothed the overly large cotton shirt over my curves. I got a little, ok a lot dazed from the feel of his warm hands on my skin. His lush lips curved. He knew the effect he had on me. "Where are your sunglasses?"

"In the back in our bunk," I replied.

"We don't have time to get them." He frowned. His were on his head. He removed them. "Here." He started to put them on me.

"No, Lucky." I waved him off. "You need them. You're the more recognizable of us. Those are your fans out there. Not mine."

"Alright, Angel." He put the Aviator shades on and reached for the ball caps. I stood still and stared into his eyes, his shaded eyes, as he wrapped my long hair around his fingers. My scalp tingled. I felt more than just mere desire when he cared for me so tenderly.

"I love the feel of your fingers in my hair."

"I love any excuse to have my hands in it or on any part of you," he informed me, his voice deliciously low as he tucked my hair into the cap and placed it on my head.

"Lucky," I breathed as all the emotions I felt for him flooded me.

"Hurry, Angel. Let's get inside the hotel. The crowd's only going to get bigger." He found and squeezed my hand, giving me a meaningful look before he released me. He put his ball cap on. It shadowed his features, but it wasn't much of a disguise. Lucky Spencer was…well… Lucky Spencer. Inky hair, piercing blue eyes, over six feet of calendar cover-worthy man, he was in my estimation the sexiest frontman out there.

"Ok. I'm ready." My lips flattened with my determination. Though I was as eager as Lucky to disembark, the jostling we had gotten after the last concert suddenly loomed large in my mind.

Those were Dragons fans outside. They were nuts for their band and understandably crazy about their lead singer. Maybe a little too crazy.

"C'mon," Lucky offered me his hand. I slid my fingers into his. Warmth and an incredible sense of security settled over me the way it always did whenever our hands were joined. He led me down the short set of stairs. I could feel the tension in his tight grip. And I heard it register in his dismay when I stepped out of the bus with him.

"Bloody hell…" The roar of the crowd drowned out the rest of his exclamation.

"Lucky! It's Lucky!" a woman in a black and red 'Get Lucky' t-shirt yelled.

"I love you!" another fan beside her screamed.

"Fuck me, Lucky!"

"Wanna get lucky with me Lucky?"

I couldn't see individuals anymore, just a wall of faces and a rush of movement coming straight toward us as we were inundated by people, most of them women in tight clothing and leather studded accessories. My body got slammed hard into Lucky's. For a brief moment I registered his warmth and scent and felt safe, but then we were ripped apart. Impatient hands shoved me backward. Fans filled into the widening gap between us. Someone elbowed me hard in the ribs. As I doubled over trying to catch my breath, another person bumped me backward and more fans rushed in pushing me further away from him. Off balance and unable to hold my ground, I tripped over a hard obstacle at my feet I couldn't even see because there were so many people pressing into me. On my way down, I caught a glimpse of Lucky. Several yards away now, he towered over the people surrounding him. I watched his lips form my name, but I couldn't hear him over all the fans screaming. He was too far away to do anything anyway. There were too many people between us. He couldn't save me this time.

CHAPTER
four

"**R**aven," Alec coaxed, his jade green eyes narrowed on my face. "Let me have a look, luv."

"It's nothing." I huddled closer beside him on the overstuffed couch in the lobby. Inside the hotel, there wasn't the massive press of humanity like out in the parking lot, but it was still pretty crowded. I was wrestling inside myself to regain my bearings after being knocked down on the pavement. I'd had to pull my arms and legs into my body to keep them from being stomped on. Thank God Alec and Cody had been nearby. They had shouldered their way in, helped me up and escorted me here. "It's only a scratch."

"I'm thinking that's not entirely true." He gently took my hand and frowned as he flipped it over.

"You're bleeding." He frowned and shook his head when he saw my knee.

"My palms are a little abraded from the pavement, and I have an insignificant cut on my knee."

"I'll be the judge of that," Alec corrected and turned to Cody who stood protectively beside us. "Get a manager. Make sure they're sending extra security to the parking lot. I'll take care of Raven." Eyes large, I watched Cody move toward the front desk and tried to convince my heartbeat to slow down. The adrenaline rush from almost being trampled still surged inside me. I knew Lucky was fine. His adoring fans wouldn't hurt him. It was him they had wanted. I had only been an unfortunate impediment on the way to reaching their goal.

"Raven." Alec carefully gathered my hands. "I'm going to find a first aid kit. Some water maybe. You look a little pale."

"I'm ok. Don't make a fuss. It's not a big deal." I swallowed to moisten my dry throat. I really didn't want him to leave me alone.

"It's going to be a big deal." He released my hands to smooth my tangled hair from my face. "Lucky's going to be furious when he sees you like this, and then he's going to be mad at me for not doing a bloody thing about it."

"You did do something. You rescued me. You and Cody both." I shoved my ripped sleeve up my shoulder, but it only slid right back down my arm again. "Lucky's not going to be angry. He's going to be grateful. I certainly am."

"Where the bloody hell is she?" Lucky stepped through the sliding glass doors practically shaking the walls as he stormed inside the lobby. Apparently he wasn't ready to be grateful just yet.

"I'm here," I squeaked. Unsticking myself from Alec's side, I stood and lifted my arm waving my hand up in the air. Lucky's gaze swept over me and his expression immediately darkened. He strode straight toward me. The people standing between us took one look at him and jumped to get of his way. The hotel security that had flanked him peeled away and moved into position at the glass doors. If only they had been around to help us a little earlier.

"Oh, Raven," he said, grabbing me by the upper arms as I swayed. "I'm so very sorry." After another quicker head to toe glance, he pulled me into him and tucked my head into his chest.

"I'm ok," I assured him.

"Are you sure, Angel?" His fingers flexed into the skin at my nape. "You don't look well." His black roadie shirt was all I saw, but I heard his dismay. It rumbled from deep inside his chest to my ear. "Shall we call the doctor?"

"No, that won't be necessary. I'm just a little shaky." And I felt a little needy. I wanted to stay right where I was with him holding me.

"I messed up badly. I'm truly sorry."

"It's ok." I wrapped my arms tighter around his waist and burrowed my cheek more into his chest, exhaling a relieved breath as he began to soothingly stroke one of his hands along the length of my spine. "I'm fine."

"I should have waited for an escort."

"We both should have. It was a mutual decision." I eased back to look up at him. His hand slipped from my hair.

"It was my fuckup. My mistake." He lifted both hands and framed my face with them. "One I won't ever repeat, I promise you." His eyes blazed cobalt flames. "No more chances. Not with you." He stroked my smooth skin with the pads of his thumbs while staring down at me. His expression became even more troubled. "When I saw you fall…" He trailed off. "And then I couldn't get to you." I felt the tremor that rolled through his solid body.

"I'm fine." And I was. Now. He had me. Pulling myself together, I loosened my death grip from his waist.

"You're not fine," he disagreed. Removing my hands from his back, he brought them to the front and shook his head as he inspected the abraded skin on my palms.

"Ok, minus getting a little scuffed up and hurting my knee." Mentioning my knee was the wrong thing to do. It made my brain focus on it. It suddenly started throbbing as if my heartbeat were centered there. I started to feel a little woozy. "Um, I think maybe I should sit down." I swayed as the fight or flight adrenaline decided fighting time was over.

"I've got you." Grasping me by my shoulders and under my knees, Lucky swept me off my feet, drawing me up into his strong arms.

"Put me down," I protested. "I'm…" I shut down my protest.

"Don't say it another time." Lucky gave me a dark look. Ok, maybe I would just stay where I was. I wrapped my arms around his neck and went with the damsel post-distress theme. "Alec," he called, turning his head to make eye contact with the bassist. "I need a room key."

"Yeah, mate." Alec moved away from the front desk and quickly crossed to join us. "They got you two in their best room, and they're sending a first aid kit straight away."

"Great. Thanks for rescuing Raven." He cleared the gravel from his voice. "I'll see that she's taken care of from here. I'm delegating the fix on this disaster to you. I want you to call Morris. Let him know exactly what happened. Don't downplay it. Tell him I want security ASAP, and that I expect it in place for tonight's show or I'm cancelling it. No more roadies pulling double duty. It's bloody unacceptable. We need real bodyguards, one for each of us and for the girls as well."

"LUCKY." I FELT my brows drawing together as I watched his Adam's apple bob. He had deposited me on the counter next to the sink in the bathroom of our suite. My feet had barely touched the floor since the lobby. I had been allowed a quick by myself shower while he had spoken with someone in the other room. But this was the second time he had examined my knee. "As you can see now that I've cleaned it off, it's really not that bad."

"I don't agree." He lifted his head. His eyes met mine. "And it never should have happened." Frowning, he stroked the uninjured skin beside the cut softly with his thumb before he flipped open the first aid kit. "Hold still, Angel." His brows creased as he located a tiny bottle of rubbing alcohol. "This is going to sting a bit."

"Alright." I placed my hands on his shoulders. He had taken off his shirt. His skin was warm satin, the tensed muscles beneath it solid steel. Within the towel I had around it, my entire body was pretty tense, too. My pulse thudded in dreaded anticipation as I watched him uncap the bottle and tip it onto a sterile pad liberally saturating it. I sucked in a sharp breath. Red hot fire blazed as he pressed the pad to my skin and the alcohol seeped into the deep crevice in my flesh.

"Sorry, Raven." He spun away and my hands fell to my sides as he threw the pad in the trash can.

"Stop saying that," I demanded.

"Stop saying you're fine then." He turned back to me, looking pensive as he stroked his long fingers up my thigh. A good distraction. The stinging began to recede.

"I will when you stop apologizing." I reached for his handsome and way too serious face. Framing it, I ran my fingers across the rough layer of overnight stubble and tipped his head up to me. "It barely even hurts anymore." I stared deeply into his eyes, hoping to make that truth register. "Stop beating yourself up about it." I knew that was what he was doing, and I willed him to let it go. "Kiss me, Lucky." Threading my fingers into his inky hair, I lifted the burdensome layers from his furrowed brow. "Take me to bed right now. Untwist my towel. Unbutton your jeans. Make love to me."

"Believe me, I'd like nothing better." His gaze dropping to my mouth, he swallowed. "You know I would." His voice a sexy rasp, his hand on my upper thigh curled into a fist. "But I need to put on the antibiotic and a bandage." He removed his hand from my leg. "And then we need to talk."

"About what?" It was my turn to swallow, my turn for my brow to crease. Trepidation swirled as I watched him reach for the tube of Neosporin. I would have much preferred he use his hands on my naked body instead.

"About what happened," he answered, saying what I was afraid he would. He slathered on a thick layer of ointment, his angled bangs arrowing more worrisome shadows into his eyes. "About how I failed you." He tore open an overly large Band-Aid.

"Oh, please." I shook my head. "You didn't fail me," I insisted as he applied the bandage. "That's ridiculous."

"But it isn't, Raven." He lifted his head, and I watched his right brow dip. His serious one. "Your safety is paramount. And I don't think you realize how bad this was or how much worse it could have been."

"I do, Lucky. C'mon. It was a little scary, but it's over now." I wished he would stop making such a big deal out of this. "We'll learn from it. We'll be more careful next time. Let's move on."

"I talked to Morris while you were in the shower."

"About security?"

"Yes. The cheap bastard said he would get back to me after he gives the matter some consideration." A muscle visibly ticked in his clenched jaw. "He doesn't get it," he bit out. "He's got no sense of urgency about it. No clue what it's really like out here for us."

"Then we'll just have to be more careful until you can convince him."

"It isn't a matter of being careful. It's about a lack of control. I put you in danger today because my priorities weren't straight."

"You wanted what I wanted. What I want right now. To be together. You making love to me in that bed. I'm going away tonight. We won't see each other for a while." We hadn't been separated since we decided to be a couple. I wasn't looking forward to it. I knew he wasn't, either. "You didn't force me to step off the bus with you."

"I want you all the fucking time, Raven. Today wasn't any different in that regard. You just getting close enough for me to get a whiff of your fragrance has me pointing north."

'Yeah, well, just looking at you is an instant turn on for me. Our feelings are intense. Don't twist that around and make it into a bad thing."

"It's bad when it results in me using poor judgment and I put you at risk like I did today." He lifted his gaze. No wide open view, his sky blue eyes were completely shuttered, his emotions locked up behind them. "I'm thinking this isn't the safest place for you to be."

"On the road with you, you mean?"

His eyes hard, he nodded once.

"But it's where I want to be." Tears pricked my eyes. "Are you saying that you want me to leave?" I tried to scoot off the counter. I suddenly felt too exposed in only a towel beneath his shuttered regard and the bright vanity lights.

"Stop, Raven." He put his hands on my shoulder, pinning me in place. "What I want has nothing to do with it. This is about doing what's best for you."

"What's best for me is being with you." I didn't want a long distance relationship. That had been a disaster for me and Ivan. How could Lucky and I move forward as a couple if we were apart? It hurt my heart that he was even considering it.

"I would have you by my side every single hour of every day if that were practical. But it's not. We both know it's not. We talked a little bit about it in LA. The road is hard. I anticipated that. I think we both did. But what I didn't foresee was the danger to you. That's on me. That oversight. What happened today is on me, too, and is ultimately my fault."

I opened my mouth to protest, but he covered it.

"It is. In our bed, in our relationship, you and I are equals, Raven." He softly stroked his thumb back and forth over my lips. "But outside of those? On the road? With this band? I'm in charge, and I'm the one responsible for the tour and everyone on it. That includes you." Dark lashes framing his resolve, he stared into my eyes imploring me to understand what he was saying and to accept it.

"Ok, Lucky," I bristled under those constraints. "You're the boss. I can accept that if that's the way you think it has to be. I can follow orders." I wasn't particularly looking forward to that type of arrangement. I wasn't a good follower, but I could be one for him if it meant I stayed and we continued with things the way they were.

"I love you. You're the perfect match for me." He tucked a strand of hair behind my ear. "That's never in doubt."

But it suddenly was. What had been certain became uncertain the moment he used the word doubt in such close proximity to such a firm declaration of his love.

"I don't want to send you away, but until we get the security situation resolved that's the way it has to be."

CHAPTER *five*

"I TRIED REASONING WITH HIM," I shook my head at Sky. Sitting beside me on the end of the bed, her fingers were clasped tightly together with mine. "He wouldn't listen."

"He'll change his mind." She sounded confident, but she had once been confident her brother would never hurt me and hurt me he had. "He's just upset." She scooted closer, her hip bumped mine and she squeezed my hands encouragingly. "You know he won't be able to stand being apart from you."

I glanced toward the bathroom where Lucky was having his turn in the shower. The door was closed. He hadn't invited me to join him. He had turned me down earlier when I had asked him to make love to me. I wasn't even gone yet, and he was already acting like I was. Inside my chest, my heart burned. I wanted to believe Sky. I wanted to believe everything would be alright, that Lucky would change his mind, but I didn't have that kind of faith. Not right now. Not with him making unilateral decisions and mandating distance between us.

Going to New York and facing Suzanne Smith's wrath now seemed a paltry concern by comparison.

"I hope you're right, Sky. But he's being really stubborn about this." My flight was in a few hours. I would continue to try to get him to reconsider, but I knew it was unlikely he would change his mind. "Thanks for bringing my things over."

"You're welcome. No trouble at all. Rocky went to the bus to get them, not me. He said things have settled down. That there's only a few diehard fans still milling about." Eyes as brilliantly blue as her brother's suddenly blurred with tears. "I'm going to miss you."

"I'll miss you, already. I enjoy spending time together." We were the only two girls on a tour bus with a bunch of rowdy guys. We had to stick together. It was a mandate in the sisterhood charter or something. "You'll have to keep them in line without me. No heavy drinking before they go on stage. Get them to eat something besides fast food once in a while. And make sure they pick up after themselves." I removed my hands from hers. "And don't forget to place an order for more 'Get Lucky' t-shirts."

"I'll try, and I will. It's on my list of things to do today. But you know the lads don't listen to me like they do you, and I'll be dreadfully bored at the merch table without you." She sighed, her breath stirring wispy strands of brown around her pretty face. "Don't be mad at Lucky." She seemed really worried, and her worry added to my stress. Did she think a temporary parting would lead to a permanent one? Did she know something I didn't? Or was this unrelated to Lucky and me? Was this because of her mother leaving her dad?

"I'm not mad exactly. More frustrated that he won't listen to me."

"He doesn't like when the people he loves get hurt."

"I know. None of us do, honey."

"Yes, but for my brother keeping the people he cares about safe is the way he expresses his love." Her delicate brow furrowed. "But keeping people from getting hurt isn't always possible, is it?"

"No." I wondered if we were still talking about her brother and me or if we had segued into why Lucky didn't want her and Rocky together.

"He used to get into fights when we were children and others said hateful things about me or Alec. Our father would get upset with him. He would say, 'Lucky, you're like Don Quixote tilting at windmills. You'll never win.'" She twisted her hands. It seemed to upset her to talk about her father. She rarely mentioned him. I don't think they had been close. Was it because he had been disappointed in her, in her unique way of processing the world? The way he had been disappointed with Lucky's choice to pursue music rather than something more practical. "I looked up the story." The crease between Sky's eyes deepened. "Don Quixote tries to defend the helpless. My brother's like that. He can't stomach people being mistreated. It's because he's kind. But you, me and Alec, we need to learn to defend ourselves. In our own way. In our own time. How can we ever be strong if we aren't given a chance to prove ourselves? Alec has Cody now. Cody doesn't care that he has to have his clothes or his food a certain way. He accepts him. He helps him only when he truly needs it. Like with the big crowd today. You have my brother. He understands and cares for you. He wants you to stay. You know in your heart he does, but he blames himself for you getting hurt today. Give him some time. He'll come around. And he might come around sooner if you find a way to show him that you can take care of yourself."

"You're right, Sky. That's good advice. Thank you. I'll try to be patient, and I'll try to find a way to prove to him that I'm capable." I gave her a shoulder nudge. "But maybe you should follow your own advice. If Rocky..." I trailed off as the door to the bathroom suddenly popped open. Caught conspiring, we both jumped a little, jostling the bed and crumpling the comforter.

Lucky emerged in a cloud of steam, his hair dripping wet and his leather pants already on for his performance, though the front strings were loosely laced. My mouth went dry. Instant turn on for sure. The frontman for the Dragons was a rock god. Not a myth. I'd fallen victim to a throng of his worshippers earlier.

"Sky." There was a question in Lucky's tone as he greeted her.

"I brought Raven her things," she explained, and he frowned. "Rocky got them from the bus. He said the Ducati is out of the trailer as you asked. It's full of petrol and in the hotel garage."

"Good." He nodded. Sky stood. I stood as well.

"I'll see you out." She gave me a puzzled look as I followed her. "I'd like to do Lucky's makeup tonight." I pulled open the door for her. "If that's ok with you?" I didn't do as good a job as she did, but I enjoyed doing it and wanted the excuse to be alone with him.

"Absolutely." She smiled a knowing smile and touched my arm softly. "That will give me more time to devote to Rocky's hammers. He never sits still long enough for me to do them properly. I'll leave accessories, makeup, everything you need in the dressing room." She stepped into the hall, and I kept the door propped open watching her until she turned the corner and disappeared from sight. My heart immediately felt heavier.

"Raven." The sad way Lucky intoned my name sounded as melancholy as I felt. His warm hands fell on my shoulders. He turned me around and the door slipped from my grip, clicking closed as he stated the obvious. "You're not dressed yet."

"I didn't feel like getting ready." I had hoped for another opportunity for him to make love to me. I lifted my hand to his neck, touching my fingertips to the upper part of his tattoo. The Chinese dragon started just below his ear and the wings spanned the width of his entire back. "Your sister says you'll miss me," I skimmed my fingers over the outline. My heart rose to my eyes as I trailed them lower along his smooth freshly shaven jawline.

"Every second of every endless day." His right brow dipped.

"I'll miss you, too." My throat flashed to soon-to-be-deprived-of-Lucky dry. "So kiss me." I tried to make my tone light. He had refused me once. I so didn't want him to refuse me now. "Make it count. There are a lot of cute actors hanging around WMO headquarters if..."

He grabbed me by the upper arms and silenced me.

His lips on mine.

Where I wanted them.

Lush Lucky bliss.

I swept my hands upward along the chiseled contours of his back, his skin still warm from his hot shower and slick because he never dried properly. His fingers digging deeper into the skin of my upper arms he crushed me into his hard chest while I grabbed fistfuls of his wet hair, twisting and tangling my fingers in the saturated strands urging him to deepen the kiss. His hot tongue pierced my mouth. I eagerly parted my lips without hesitation. I wanted him to taste me, to have and consume me. I didn't want this to be about who had control. I wanted it to be about us and the wildness he made me feel all the way to the chaotic end.

I didn't get what I wanted.

He ripped his mouth from mine. He was breathing hard. I felt the cost of his restraint. His rigid chest sawed over my breasts. His gaze was bright, his skin hot as he pressed our foreheads together, his eyes swallowed in darkness like the last hour before midnight. "No actors, Raven. No other guys. You're mine, and mine alone. I won't tolerate anyone else touching you. That part of our story is history."

CHAPTER
Six

WE TOOK LUCKY'S DUCATI TO THE VENUE. I wrapped my arms around his waist and held on tight though traffic was light and the downtown streets were mostly deserted. I didn't want to let go of him. I didn't want to leave. I wanted to be his and only his with no space at all between us. But he was sending me away, and the part of our story we both wanted to end was waiting for me on the other side of a two hour flight.

Rock Fuck Club was far from over.

Lucky parked the bike, removed his helmet, helped me with mine and took my hand leading me toward the building. His grip was so tight it practically cut off my circulation. Was it finally starting to hit him—that time might be running out for us?

The Tabernacle was a church that had been converted into a music venue. Lucky had never played in the club before, but that didn't slow him down. He followed the directional signs. Handwritten in the past, they were typed and printed on expensive card stock now. An example of the new tour perks like having two buses, one for the band and the other for the manager and roadies. Besides being mobbed by rabid fans, the rapid rise of the Dragons showed in a lot of ways.

I stutter stepped and stopped when we entered the performance hall, taking in the breathtaking space. Gleaming hardwood floors beneath my feet. Soaring domed ceiling overhead. Ornate details abounded. Two balconies and arches framed a former organ behind the elevated stage. It was super cool and large and the Dragons had sold it completely out, all twenty six hundred tickets. I hated that I was going to miss their show tonight. And the next one. Who knew how many more? I had been kicked off the tour. Would Lucky ever allow me to return to it?

"Lucky," Alec called. He stood on the left side of the stage and strummed a couple of test chords on his Fender. "Hustle up." The rest of the band was getting ready for sound check, too. On the right, Cody had his guitar. Rocky was on the riser with his drums. The Dragons lacked only one.

"I need to go." Lucky spun me in front of him and pressed a soft kiss to my slightly parted lips. "Don't wander too far." He unthreaded our joined fingers and untethered me.

"Go. They need you." I let him go, pretending the separation didn't make my chest hurt. "Don't worry about me. I'll find your sister and check on her." And I wanted to find that piano. Sure my palms were abraded from the fall, but I felt like I needed my fingers on the ivory and ebony to exorcise some of my melancholy. Get my emotions out in the open where I could process and try to make sense of them. Creating music had always been cathartic for me. Lucky and I had that in common. Mine had been dammed up inside of me until he had come along and helped me reopen the floodgates.

Lucky gave me a grateful look before he jogged away. I watched him, reluctant to let him go even visually. The maroon button down shirt with the botanical print flowed freely across his wide shoulders like the rivulets of water had after his shower. Though it lent a vintage vibe to his already compelling appearance, I knew he would shed it before taking the stage later tonight. Another something I would miss. My gaze dropped lower to his ass in his black leather pants. That view held me captive for a couple of additional beats. And then there was his cocky stride. Where his best friend walked with precision and economy, Lucky glided, his movements so smooth and rhythmic I could almost hear the soundtrack that must have been playing inside his head.

When he reached the stage, Lucky took the stairs to the top two at a time. He took his guitar from his guitar tech and strapped it on. Noticing me, not that he could he miss me standing in the center of the hall, star struck as I was by him, he gave me a chin lift of acknowledgement and went straight to work. Lucky might not give Charles Morris every little concession the CEO of Zenith Productions wanted when he wanted it, but he gave his fans all he had to give every single night. He would never let them down. His habit was to lead the guys through at least a couple of bars of each song on their set list. Once upon a time when I had first seen the Dragons I had thought they needed polishing. I didn't think that anymore.

I watched the first song pass the lead singer's muster. On the next, he had Cody tighten his chords. The second run through showed a notable improvement. Lucky had a keen ear. It would be a letdown, a major one, to miss the payoff tonight in front of a real audience.

Feet dragging my heavy heart with them, I turned and went to find Sky. I didn't have far to go. She was on the other side of the hall in the ornate lobby. The merch area was just to the right in a small alcove at the top of a carpeted staircase. Knowing there was a lot more to set up now that her designs and the guys' slogans had been incorporated into t-shirts, key chains, stickers and silicon concert bracelets, I got right to work alongside her, opening up the bins and helping her arrange everything.

"Hey," I said when we were finished. "I'm gonna take off and explore." I acted nonchalant as if Lucky's voice drifting to us from the adjacent hall didn't send chills up my spine. "You gonna be ok by yourself for a while?"

"You know I will be." She gave me a firm look. "I can take care of myself." Apparently my gentle nudge had taken hold.

I gave her an approving nod.

"I left everything you need for Lucky in the dressing room. It's the third door down the hall behind the stage. I noticed it has a lock on the door." Her eyes sparkled. I think she well suspected what I had planned. I wondered if she knew the whole of it. I was going to attempt to use sex to leverage Lucky into keeping me on the tour. "I'll do the guys' makeup out here and keep them away as long as I can, but you can't do his makeup. He wants to take you to the airport on the Ducati. His helmet would smear everything. But you could do something else if you'd like. I've been trying for ages to get him to paint his nails black."

"That would look cool when he's onstage wearing all of his silver rings."

"I thought so, as well, but he's been resistant. Maybe you can convince him."

"I'll try." I squeezed her hand to confirm, then I scooted through the six inch gap between the counter and the wall. I knew exactly how long sound checks lasted. I had thirty minutes of time to kill.

I continued down a long hall, turned right down another one and found the piano waiting in a ten by ten foot space right next to the dressing room. The shelves beside it were lined with songbooks. The church's pianist had probably used the room for lessons. I closed the door and pulled out the bench. The piano, a glossy upright, played like a dream. Lost in the new melody that sounded so much better on an actual piano than it had on the band's keyboard, I didn't hear the timer on my cell go off. I also didn't hear Lucky come in until I saw his reflection in the high gloss finish. He leaned against the door jamb with one booted foot casually hooked over the other. He beckoned me to come to him with a single crook of his first finger. I closed the piano, stood and crossed to him refitting myself to his side. His hands settled on my hips. He gazed down at me without speaking as if he didn't want to spoil the moment with words and was savoring the view of my face. I was certainly staring at him and doing the same.

"We've got a dressing room all to ourselves," I said after the moment stretched on and I remembered how little time we had left. "Sky's going to do the guys' makeup at the merch booth." His eyes flared. Apparently, the idea of having some privacy excited him, too. "We didn't have time to say goodbye properly earlier, and I wondered if you might like to do that."

"Lead the way," he cut in before I could ramble more. So I did. I didn't need a directional sign to know where to go. It was just a matter of stepping back out into the hall and dipping into the next room. But a deeper meaning hit me and gave me pause because I knew that when it came to him I didn't require any instruction at all. I loved him. My heart was meant to be his, and I would take him anyway I could get him. Sure, it would be stressful trying to find the right groove for our relationship given the lifestyles we both led. But no matter how crowded or crazy it got there was no other place I would rather be than by his side. No other man I wanted but him. My heart had known almost from the beginning that he was the one, though it had taken my brain a little while to reach that conclusion so soon after Ivan's betrayal.

"No. Absolutely not." Lucky shook his head when he saw the table and the bottles of nail polish lined up beside his leather necklace, bracelets and rings. "No way."

"Aw, c'mon," I coaxed. "Your sister thinks it would be really cool, and so do I. Why don't we give it a try? If you don't like the way it looks, it's easy to remove."

"I can think of better things to do with twenty minutes," he growled.

"So can I." A shiver rolled through me. We had learned to be fast and creative on this tour. Behind speakers. In storage closets. Lucky could make me come twice in the amount of time we had left. "If we get started I can do the polish *and* whatever else you would like." I wanted to do this, wanted him to remember me every time he looked down at his hands. Plus, I wanted an opportunity to tell him everything that was inside my heart.

"Alright, let's do it." He took a seat across from me as he picked up the jewelry and put it on. The long leather necklace he doubled around his neck twice. The assortment of heavy silver bracelets he fastened to his wrists. "But matte black only, no glitter or sparkles."

"Ok." My lips twitched as I watched him slide the lion's head ring on his index finger and the coin edged one on his thumb. "I can make that concession. I'm willing to negotiate." I reached for the matte black bottle and met his gaze across the table. "Compromise is supposed to be good for relationships, you know."

"Raven," he warned, his expression hard. "That discussion is closed. You go until it's safe for you to return. It's not up for debate."

"Licorice shade no sparkle it is." The thickness in my voice betrayed my disappointment. I swallowed to loosen the tangle, realizing that the little chance I thought I might have to change his mind before I left was actually none. Blinking to clear the burn from my gaze, I shook the bottle of polish, unscrewed the lid, pulled out the wand and wiped off the excess on the glass rim. "Give me your hand, please." His gaze on mine he stretched out his arm and extended his hand. I took it, stroking the underside with my thumb. His ice blue eyes darkened to a deep sapphire. My breath caught on the longing that swelled inside my chest. "You'll need to keep it steady for me."

"I can keep it steady all night long."

I arched a brow. "I know you can." Lowering my gaze, I focused on his hand. His nails were blunt edged and nicely trimmed. I felt the electrical hum I always felt when we touched.

"I love how you do that." He felt it, too, that awareness, the desire vibrating between us.

"Do what?" I lifted my gaze and pretended not to understand as I continued to caress his skin with the pad of my thumb under the pretense of separating his fingers for the polish.

"Look deeply into my eyes like you are right now while touching me that way."

"Oh." My cheeks flushed. "I'm glad you love it." I lowered my gaze, brushed on four careful strokes on his first finger and paused to admire it. "It's a compulsion. I can't help myself when I'm with you." He had his ways of expressing his love, and I had mine. I returned the wand to the bottle, dipped it, reduced the excess and started on his thumb.

"It's sexy like you are, Angel." His approval and the deep rumble of his voice lit a roaring fire in the hearth of my heart. "Don't ever stop."

"I won't." Didn't he know that I couldn't stop? Bottom lip between my teeth, I refocused and brushed a couple of strokes onto his thumb, then got more polish and went to work on his middle finger. Slender and long, my breath caught as I held it. In our bunk, not even hours ago, he'd had that finger inside me. Remembering, I overshot the edge of his nail and had to use my own to scrape away the polish from his skin.

"Raven." He lifted my chin. "What were you thinking just now?"

"I was thinking about you." I met his gaze, and his question unflinchingly. "What your finger feels like when you slide it inside me." I felt the sudden stillness in him. I held my breath as I brushed my thumb along the length of his middle digit while holding his gaze.

"Raven. Fuck." The blaze in his eyes incinerated me.

"You always know just how to move it." I gave him my sultry tone. "And you always apply just the right amount of pressure in just the right spot." I knew what I was doing. Teasing. Titillating. But I pretended I didn't hear his heavy breathing or the thundering of my own heartbeat. I dropped my gaze, dipped the applicator, swiped off the excess and moved to his ring finger. I brushed on more polish. Then I finished his pinky. One hand done, I returned the wand to the bottle.

"What do you think?" I lifted my gaze, but he wasn't looking at the black nails on his sexy hand, that in my opinion just cranked his rock star amp up to eleven. He was staring at me, and his gaze was heated.

"I'm thinking time's up in the nail salon." He threw back his chair. "And that you're about to get shagged."

"You'll mess up your polish." I jumped back from the table as he stalked me, his intention clear.

"Don't care."

"You're in leather pants. Those are hard to get off," I reminded him, remembering our first time in Boston.

"No need to take them all the way off, Angel." He was directly in front of me now. We were less than an inch apart. I could feel his heat. It rolled off him in tantalizing waves.

Yes, now, please. "Do it then," I challenged. "What are you waiting for?"

"At your service, Angel." He plunged the hand I hadn't yet painted into my hair. He yanked my face up to his. He nipped me with the edge of his teeth before his tongue invaded my mouth. Rapid thrusts. Hard thrusts. Deep ones, he kissed me like he planned to fuck me. And I was totally with him. My hands rushed all over him. Sculpted arms. Solid chest. His smooth skin. Everywhere I could reach, I memorized with my touch. My legs trembled when he broke the seal between our lips.

"Get ready," he warned, walking me backward until my retreat ended at a wall. "For more than just my finger." His sensual lips curled. His eyes pierced mine. "But since I fancy the polish, you'll have to get me ready. Unlace my pants," he ordered in a commanding tone I couldn't resist.

"Alright." I smoothed my hands down his narrow hips and long legs as I lowered myself to the floor. The concrete was cold beneath my bent knees even through my jeans, but his heated gaze warmed me. My mouth went dry as I reached for him and traced his exquisite length. He hissed in a sharp breath. I glanced up, met his gaze and licked my lips while I slowly unlaced the front of his leather pants. He shuddered when I freed him.

"Up, temptress." He had to tug on my hair to get me to stand. "I know what you're thinking, but I wouldn't last longer than three seconds with your wet lips around my cock." His eyes glittered. "You wanted to play, It's time to play." He took my mouth, wet and raw, no holding back this time. I loved it. I was panting when he released me. "Get your jeans undone." He stamped his hands to the wall on either side of my head. "Now," he growled, staring at me, his gaze dark as he watched me lower my zipper. "Thong, too. To your thighs. That's far enough." He adjusted his hips. The head of his cock nudged me between my legs. I reached for it. I wanted to touch him, wanted to run my fingers along his satiny hot steely length. I wanted him inside me. His lids lowered as I stroked him firmly from root to tip the way I knew he liked it. "That feels good." He peered at me through the thick fringe of his lashes. "Going to put it in you now, Angel. Make it good for both of us. Turn around. Hands on the wall."

I complied, and he gathered my tee, lifted it up baring my skin to the middle of my back and smoothed his palm over my flesh. "Be a good girl. Brace and bend for me."

"Lucky," I breathed, being a good girl and doing what he wanted, what I wanted. I was so exposed in this position, so turned on, so ready. "Please."

"You have such a lovely round ass, Raven." He grabbed my hips in his strong grip, yanked me backward and rammed his entire length inside me. My feet still in my shoes skidded forward from the force of his entry. I hissed from the pleasure-pain, a stinging and a stretching from his thick cock that felt so good. "You're so wet, so tight around me." He made an approving humming sound, gliding smoothly nearly all the way out until only the head remained then sliding back inside me.

I moaned. He was so big, and he filled me so good. His grip tightened on the skin at my hips. He picked up the pace, deepening the penetration and fucking me so hard he lifted me onto the tips of my toes.

"Lucky, yes!" My hands braced on the wall, I took what he gave. In and out he went over and over again. My skin got all warm and shivery. My cunt was completely soaked. I surfed the crest of pleasure as he pounded his hard cock into me. "So good," I praised as he thrust inside. "You feel so good. Don't stop. Please don't stop. I'm so close."

He didn't talk. Breathing hard, he fucked me harder. Deeper. Faster. He took me right there. Straight to the edge. I careened along it. He stiffened, and I sailed right off with him. Freefalling. Chanting his name. No net. No fear of the future. Just the here and now and this pure, hot, decadent pleasure.

CHAPTER
seven

I TURNED MY HEAD TO RECEIVE THE proprietary kiss he pressed to my lips. Lushness. Warmth. Perfection.

He pulled out, stepped away and returned with some tissues. I cleaned up while he refastened the ties on his pants. He watched me closely as I straightened my clothes and finger combed my hair into a long French braid. My cell went off from where I had left it on the table. A reminder notification. My chest tight, I crossed to my phone, unlocked it and shut the reminder off before it could ring again.

"What was the alarm for?"

"My flight." My gaze lifted to meet his. "I was afraid I might get distracted."

"You were right." He eliminated the space between us. He placed his large hands low on my hips. I'd have bruises there from what we had done tomorrow. But I had absolutely zero regrets. Knowing I drove him wild made me wild. The afterglow of lovemaking with Lucky usually made me smile, but now I felt a dismayed frown threatening to form. "It's time for you to go, Angel."

"Not yet." Sadness. Resignation. Helplessness. My heart hurt. Love shouldn't feel like this.

"But Raven..." He trailed off as I covered his mouth with my fingers. Renewed desire flooded me when he pressed his lush lips to my skin. But I had to set passion aside. I had indulged that need. Now it was time for the rest. "That was only the first alarm. I programmed a second one. I want to finish your polish." I stretched my arm out gesturing to the table. "Sit back down." That frown I'd been holding back broke out when he didn't move. "You know it'll drive Alec nuts if you go out on stage tonight with only one hand painted. It won't take long."

"Sky can do it." He was putting me off.

"Your sister has plenty of other things to do. We need to talk."

"We can talk on the phone when I can't touch you."

"We can. I hope we do. But I need to talk to you *and* touch you for these last few minutes we have together."

"Alright, Raven." His brow dipped as he grabbed the back of the chair. He turned it around backwards and straddled it, sinking slowly onto it bringing images to mind that made me hot and shivery again. The effect was magnified by his heated gaze.

"Stop looking at me like that, Lucky. You know we don't have that kind of time anymore."

"I would rather have our last few moments together spent doing something enjoyable."

It hurt my heart that he was trying so hard to avoid this conversation. Breaking the connection between our gazes, I tried to regroup my thoughts as I took a seat in the chair opposite him. "Hand, please," I requested, head bowed to hide the flood of emotion in my eyes.

"Angel, I don't care to argue." He made a preemptive attempt to cut off the protest he knew I was going to make. "Don't be upset. You have to admit this is the way it must be."

"Of course I'm upset. And no I don't agree that this is the way it has to be." I took his hand without looking up. Amid the graffiti on the table, that very masculine hand could have been an advertisement for a rock 'n roll jewelry company.

Go through the motions, Raven. Do what needs to be done. I reached for the polish, shook it, twisted open the lid, withdrew the wand and wiped off the excess. Applicator ready, words in my mouth, it was time to speak them. Caressing his thumb like I had before, I lifted my gaze and got rocked just looking at him. At his inky dark tousled hair. Into those gorgeous sky-blue eyes framed by those thick black sooty lashes. But Lucky was more than a collection of handsome features. He was the sum of everything I always needed.

"We're at an impasse, you and me. I want to stay, and you're making me go." I painted his thumb.

"It's not safe for you. We went over this already, Raven."

"I know we did. But I need things to be clear. We've been together as a couple for a while, and now we're going to be apart." I went for more polish, dipped, swiped and returned to his hand. Four strokes before I lifted my gaze. His lids were lowered, his eyes partially shuttered. "What are your expectations for me in the interim? For us?"

"You mean for our relationship?"

"Yes."

"I expect our relationship to go on, of course." His expression turned hard. "Don't you?"

"Yes, it's what I want more than anything. But how can it work with you out here on the road and me miles away in New York? What happens after I meet with Suzanne Smith? Where do I go then? Where do you want me to go?" I lowered my gaze, went for more polish repeating the procedure and returned to apply polish to his middle finger. A protracted silence descended like a heavy curtain. I painted his nail, held my breath and lifted my gaze.

"That's a lot of questions I don't have precise answers for." Shadows, there were so many shadows inside his eyes. Burdens. Regrets. "I need time to work out the logistics. Are you saying you need to know now?"

"I've done the separation from a boyfriend thing before. It didn't turn out well. I don't want to go through that again. If I agree to it, I need to know exactly what I'm in for." I felt the change in him. I could see it in his eyes.

"I'm not Ivan Carl." His tone was as chilling as his gaze.

"I know you're not." Ice dripped down my spine as I went for more polish. "But you have to admit the situations are similar." No hiding. No games. I put it all out there for him to see. "Worst case scenario. What if you never think it's safe for me to return to the tour?" I lowered my eyes, afraid so very afraid to push him right now. But our relationship was too vital to me not to clarify.

"You want me to decide our entire future? Right here? Right now?"

"Yes." I froze solid.

"Based on a hypothetical?"

"Yes." I re-dipped the wand. I swiped. I finished his hand. I stroked his skin with my thumb. My chest was so tight now I could barely breathe. When I lifted my gaze, I found myself rocked again, only this time in a not so good way. He was angry.

"You do realize how unreasonable this sounds, Angel. How impertinent?" He withdrew his hands. His abrupt motion rattled the table. The bottle of polish spilled. I watched the inky black puddle spread. I gulped around the sudden knot in my throat. It felt like a bad omen.

"I didn't mean it to be demeaning." I pushed back from the table, too. I stood and wrapped my arms around myself. "I was only sharing a legitimate concern. I have a right to ask. You know I don't like uncertainty." It swirled around me, between us like an invisible shield.

"What in the bloody hell do you think it means when I tell you every single day how much I love you?" His gaze was as unwavering as his words. "And today when I told you I would spend every minute with you if I could? And that your safety is paramount?"

"I'm sorry." His certainty rattled the shield. "I shouldn't let what happened to me in my past color our relationship." His eyes remained icy, but there was some thawing. "But you're asking a lot of me." My lips trembled.

"Raven." He came close and lifted my chin. His rings were cold against my skin as he stroked my cheek. "The circumstances might be similar, but the players are different. Don't you know me well enough by now to know you can trust me? That you can trust where this is going between us?"

LUCKY FLIPPED ON the Ducati turn indicator. I laid my head against his leather jacket, tightened my hold around his waist and pressed my body deeper into his. Not because the ramp was particularly steep, but because we were at the exit for the Atlanta Hartsfield Airport and because my life was about to take a sharp turn. He would drop me off in a couple of minutes and nothing was resolved between us.

I had to trust him or not.

It was all on me.

And I was feeling far from confident.

The tearful goodbyes with Sky and the guys had only added to the jumble of my emotions. I didn't want to leave. And I was worried about what Suzanne Smith had planned for me. No Lucky by my side this time. No Marsha, either. No Sky. None of my new family to lend me their support. I was wondering if that walk under the arch in Monument Valley had worked. Right now it didn't feel like I was starting a future clear from the taint of my past.

We came to a stop sign. Lucky brought the Ducati to a halt and dropped his heavy biker boots to the pavement. I watched a couple of people with their roller suitcases cross in front of us. The sign for departures lay straight ahead. It was almost time to say goodbye.

Lucky twisted the throttle giving the engine some gas and zipped us into a spot a large SUV had vacated. At the curb, he turned the motor off. I reached for the strap beneath my chin, but I couldn't get it to release. My hands were shaking too badly. I cursed under my breath.

"Raven." He kicked the stand down, put his feet on the ground and turned his head. "Hold onto me. Get off the bike first. Then remove your helmet."

Yeah, that would work. Only I wondered whether or not I could really let go of him.

But I did what I had to, and he dismounted after me. Once I got the stupid helmet off, I tried to duck my head, but I was a beat too slow.

"Don't cry, Angel." He had seen the telltale sheen misting my eyes. He doffed his own helmet and shook out his hair.

"I'm not crying," I lied.

He took my helmet from my lax grip and set it on the sidewalk beside his. I was so far gone that seeing them side by side made the tears I had been attempting to hold back rush down my cheeks. In a matter of moments, he would get on the Ducati and go back to his life without me.

"Hey." He framed my face in his warm hands. "No need for tears." He brushed aside the wetness with his thumbs. "We'll find a solution."

But when? I wondered. The Dragons had an upcoming stop in Jersey, close enough to New York for me to see him again. Would he allow me to rejoin the tour there or would that end up being yet another painful goodbye?

"I know it's not the end of the world." I lifted my chin. Only it felt that way. "It's just that…I mean…That you are…oh, hell." I gave up, grabbed his arms and planted my face in his jacket.

"It's alright, Angel." He stroked his hands up and down my back. But the leather of my jacket was too thick. I wanted to feel the warmth of his touch, the connection of his skin to mine.

"You're right, of course it will be," I managed after a couple of in and out breaths of his soothing mandarin and spice scent. "I'm sorry." I unzipped my jacket and handed it to him, trying to pretend I didn't see the sympathy in his eyes. "I didn't mean to fall apart like this." I told myself to focus on how adorable he looked with his hair helmet smushed and not on how much my chest hurt. "It's just that being with you, going to sleep with you and then waking in your arms, I've gotten accustomed to it. And leaving you, it feels all wrong."

"Oh, Raven, I fancy having you around, as well." He squeezed his eyes shut. After a long beat, he reopened them. They surface of his gaze sparkled like an aquamarine gemstone. "I'll miss those things you mentioned, too." His voice was gruff. "I'll miss you. I can put up with the bullshit that goes along with this job just knowing that I have you to look forward to at the beginning and at the end of every day. I hope you know that."

I did know, but it lightened my heart for him to remind me. "I don't want to add to your stress." I lifted my hands to his handsome face and smoothed the vertical slash between his brows with my thumbs. Then I skimmed my fingers down the length of his nose and along his jaw. I lingered when I reached the lushness of his lips. Brushing my thumbs back and forth over the warm satiny texture of them, I stared deeply into his eyes. "This day went by too fast. I wish we had more time."

"I wish we did, too."

"So, this isn't goodbye." My throat closed. "Just a see you later." I started to turn away, but he grabbed me by my wrists, lifting one of my hands to his mouth to press a tender kiss to the sensitive underside and then did the same to the other. Fresh tears sprang to my eyes.

"You do what you need to do to appease Smith." His gaze was as unwavering as the command. "I'll do my part to resolve the problems on my end. The sooner we can get back to being you and me together again the better."

CHAPTER
eight

I STARED OUT THE WINDOW WATCHING THE workers bustling around on the drizzle dampened tarmac. Inside the plane we were waiting for the flight crew to give the go ahead for us to get off. But my mind wasn't on the activity around me. I was thinking about those I had left behind like I had been during most of the flight.

Had Sky already done the guys' makeup by now?

Did Rocky finally stay still long enough for her to get his hammer mask just right?

Did Sky pick up on his physical cues this time? His rapid breaths? his darkened eyes? Did she really not realize that the reason he was so restless during those sessions was because her touch turned him on?

What about Cody and Alec? Had Alec messed with Cody's supply of guitar pics again? The bassist liked them lined up on his mic pole for easy access, and he had to have them exactly evenly spaced. But the rhythm guitarist enjoyed ruffling his lover's compulsive feathers.

And Lucky. A big sigh. How many women waited for him beside

the stage door tonight? They would give him anything he wanted. Would any tempt him? He wasn't Ivan Carl. I knew that. He would end it with me before he slept with anyone else. But how long would it be before that happened? How many nights before his honor gave way to easy access? Certainty was elastic. When we were together, it was the binding that held us close, but it didn't feel as sure when stretched long distance. How long before it snapped in the middle? And how badly hurt would I be when it did?

"Miss Winters," the first class flight attendant prompted with a careful smile. "Is everything alright?"

"Yes." What total bullshit. I wasn't even close to alright.

"Is there anything else I can get you? The other passengers have already left."

"I'm sorry. I didn't notice. Lost in my thought." Slogging through a morass of confusion and doubt without him. "I just need to get my bag." I unlatched my belt, scooted past the only other seat in my row and grabbed my duffle from the overhead bin. It was light. I had left the bulk of my wardrobe behind in my Dallas apartment. There wasn't a lot of extra storage space on the bus. I didn't need much on the road. Flip flops or sneakers. Jeans. Dragon t-shirts or ones from other bands I had picked up along the journey. I modified them with Sky's help, widening the necks, fraying the hem, making them my own while at the same time creating a wearable memory. I often re-wore the same clothes. I didn't stay in them long enough for them to get dirty. I spent most of my time naked, curtain drawn, in the bunk I shared with Lucky.

I mumbled a thank you to the flight attendant and trudged up the gangway. Hitching my duffle higher on my shoulder, I considered how I would get to WMO. A taxi, I guessed. Uber didn't work in the city. It would have been nice if the big multimedia conglomerate had prearranged transportation for me, and perhaps they had. I withdrew my cell from my cross body purse and went to my settings, taking it off airplane mode. It searched for a connection and started pinging alerts as soon as I stepped inside the terminal. I didn't notice any messages from WMO, but there were several from him.

Lucky: Remember to call when you land

Lucky: The ride to the Tabernacle sucked without you. No riding the Ducati until you return.

Lucky: I keep expecting to see you. On the bus. In the dressing room. Waiting for me beside the stage.

Lucky: Were my instructions unclear? Your flight has landed. Why haven't you called me?

The overly taut feeling inside my chest eased as I read them. I was just about to call him when someone spoke my name.

"Raven."

A familiar voice. One that made happy tears prick my eyes. I turned to scan for her, but it wasn't necessary. Her long blond hair trailing behind her, she came barreling at me at the speed of let's-be-first-in-line-for-a-Fletcher's-corndog-at-the-Texas-state-fair-the-minute-it-opens. In other words, superfast. I barely had time to brace. She rocked me back on my flip-flops as she threw her arms around me. My duffle strap sliding down to the crook of my arm, I returned her embrace. When I peeled back to look at her, my smile was as bright as hers.

"Marsha." I hugged her again, tighter.

"Can't breathe," she gasped.

"I missed you." I loosened my hold somewhat.

"I'm getting the idea." She eased back, took my hands and gave me a wry look. "Missed you more." She shushed me when I opened my mouth to protest. "Don't argue. You know it's true. You have Lucky."

Yeah, I had him now, but for how long? Ours wasn't like the relationship Marsha and I shared. We were a one plus one time tested institution.

"Alright." I slid the strap of my bag back up my shoulder. "But you're not completely alone. You have your dad. Your brothers."

"My father prefers to ignore me. I prefer to do the same." She glanced away. She and her dad had a complicated relationship, one that had grown even more complicated after her mother had disappeared. "My brothers only stop by to see me now because they know I have some money from WMO." She threw her hair over her slim shoulder in a dismissive gesture like neither of those things mattered to her, but I knew they did.

I framed her face in my hands. "What are you doing here?"

"I'm here to see you. Isn't that obvious?"

"But how? Why?"

"I called your man. He told me what was going on and gave me your flight info. And *voilà* I'm here because you need me." She hesitated. "Don't you?"

"You know I do." I hugged her again. She returned my hug then set me back, her hands on my shoulders, a familiar mischievous twinkle in her gaze.

"So here we are. You and me. In New York City. The town that never sleeps. And we are completely unsupervised." She grinned. "So let's get wild and crazy, and make it count. What do you want to do first?"

I TRIED CALLING Lucky on the taxi ride into Manhattan. It rolled directly to voicemail, but the sound of his recorded voice made my breath hitch. My imagination immediately went where it shouldn't as I noted the time.

He's just at the VIP meet and greets, I told myself preparing to leave a light and breezy message after the beep. "Lucky," I greeted. "I got your texts. I'm on the way into the city. Marsha's here. She found me as soon as I got off my plane. Thank you for telling her where I would be. Call whenever you have a moment free." My throat tightened. "I love you."

"Aww," Marsha commented. I could see her studying me out of the corner of my eye. I wanted to twist my hands together, but I kept my turmoil internal.

Everything is going to be ok, I told myself.

"But enough with the mushy stuff." She patted my knee. "He's there. We're here. And I guess it's up to me to choose where we start this party since you seem to be having trouble getting on board with the Texas girls running amok in Manhattan train."

"Alright." I leaned back into my seat, refusing to believe that the shadows from the bridge's girders were an omen. "So what's first, my crazy compadre?" I turned to glance at her raising a brow.

"Drinks, duh." She smiled at me, her blue eyes blindingly bright. She was a balm to me. She warmed my soul. "There's an Irish bar by the Empire State building. TripAdvisor says it's pretty cool. After that we can do the whole touristy thing. Greenwich Village. Soho. Rockefeller Center. Staten Island."

Both my brows rose. "That's an ambitious agenda."

"Hey, we were in and out of the city so fast the last time we didn't get to see any of the highlights."

"I don't have a problem with it. Sounds fun but it's not exactly mayhem."

"Ok, so we'll start with the crazy tonight, sleep in late, then do the other more mundane stuff in the morning. We'll cover all our bases. Sound good?"

"Sounds great." I cover her hand with my own and squeezed it while holding her gaze. Connected to my bestie again, she steadied my out of sync groove.

My cell suddenly rang. It wasn't the ring tone I had programmed for Lucky, but my heart took flight anyway. Maybe he was calling me from a venue phone.

"Hello," I answered, my voice noticeably breathy with anticipation.

"Miss Winters," a young feminine voice chimed like a crystal bell. She sounded vaguely familiar.

"Yes, it is. How can I help you?"

"I don't know if you remember me. But it's Barbara. Barbara Michaels. Suzanne Smith's secretary. She had me track your flight. I know it's after-hours, and I apologize in advance but Ms. Smith expects you to come straight to her office." She mumbled under her breath. "Working late again." She sighed. "Are you in the city yet?"

"Yes." Were they tracking my cell, too? Kinda creepy. "Our taxi just drove over the bridge."

"So you're thirty minutes away. Ms. Smith is sending me out to get her a coffee. Would you like me to get you one as well?"

"Yes, thank you." That was thoughtful of her, but even so my heart plummeted knowing the meeting I had hoped to avoid until tomorrow was already here. "And make it two. Marsha West is coming with me." I was going to need all the support I could get. I knew Suzanne Smith better than I wanted to. It was going to be a late night, and it was going to be anything but fun.

CHAPTER
nine

"WELCOME BACK TO NEW YORK." The formidable exec lifted her gaze as Barbara stepped ahead of us into her corner office to announce us. "Sit down. We need to get started." She set aside the papers she had been perusing and stretched out her hand to indicate the leather and chrome chairs in front of her desk. More like the hot seats. Marsha and I had been in them before. It wasn't an experience that I relished repeating.

"Thank you, Miss Michaels." She dipped her chin to acknowledge the white and green to go cup with the protective sleeve that her assistant placed in front of her. "That will be all for now."

The blond with her hair pulled back in a severe chignon like her boss' mouthed a silent 'good luck' to me on her way out. Before it could settle in that we might have an ally in a place I never expected to have one, Smith addressed me.

"You made good time from the airport." She settled back into her cream colored high-backed chair and picked up a pen. "La Guardia's unpredictable these days with all the construction." She rolled her expensive-black and probably real gold writing instrument back and forth between her perfectly manicured but ring-free hands. "And speaking of blowing hot and cold. She leaned forward and taped her pen to the stack of papers atop her desk. "Here you two are."

I recognized my signature and Marsha's on the top of the stack.

I could see that we were going to get right to it. No segue. No build up. Right to the throat. I straightened my spine and braced for the barrage. Suzanne Smith more than held her own in an industry full of alphas. I knew better than to appear to be weak.

"We'll start with you, Miss Winters." The exec's hazel-green eyes remained as raptor sharp as I remembered. "You sat in that very same chair not long ago and promised me eight more episodes, eight more cities, eight more rockers. You went on record denying a relationship with the Dragons' lead singer. I emphasized that you had to be perceived as a player for the series concept to work. I made it clear that it was nonnegotiable." She narrowed her gaze. "Yet, you ignored my directives. You lied to me."

"We filmed eight cities and rockers." My voice wasn't as firm as I wished.

"Technically, yes. I've been going over the footage with my team and the beta-watchers. I'll get to my observations in a moment. But I'll tell you upfront that I consider you to be in material breach of your contract."

Dread pooled in the pit of my stomach.

"So the question is how are you planning to make amends?"

"I'm here. I take full responsibility for my actions." I didn't want Marsha to get into trouble, and I also remembered Lucky's directive to do whatever it took to appease Smith.

"There were two of us when we started Rock Fuck Club," Marsha added firmly. "And the two of us together will make things right." She glanced at me, and we exchanged a firm nod.

"Excellent. So are you both prepared to return the funds you received from my company plus the customary reparation of one and half times that amount for damages?"

Holy fuck!

"Um, no. I mean I could return most of the advance I received." It was relatively untouched, less what I had given to my best friend to cover her debts. "But I don't have anything beyond that."

"I only have the salary I was given for being a production assistant." Marsha turned as white as the legal documents looming on the exec's desk.

"Well. Then we're left to salvage this mess. Something I'm not overly fond of doing." She shook her head. "It's certainly not what I envisioned at the beginning when Barbara first outlined the Rock Fuck Club proposal."

"Barbara?" My brows rose. "You mean your secretary?"

"Don't look so surprised." She nodded. "Barbara has a background in music. She's very tuned in on social media trends. In our line of work it pays to know what's happening in real time and to act quickly and decisively." She made a tsking sound. "Usually. In this instance we'll just have to see how things play out after I view the final product." She pinned me with an expectant look.

"What do you mean?" I squirmed in my chair. "What more is there to do?"

"We must re-film certain scenes."

"Which ones?" I gulped.

"The vignettes with the other members of the Dragons, of course. Not to mention the one with Spencer himself."

"We're redoing entire episodes?" I croaked.

"No. Not entirely." She rolled her pen again and honed her predatory gaze on me. "The one with the drummer, Mr. Harris will only need a partial redo. BDSM is a popular fantasy. It's sexy the way you both portrayed it, but it's not enough. Viewers need to see some kissing, some tenderness, some actual aftercare on camera."

"Ok, I guess." Lucky had said to do whatever it took to make the boss happy, but he also made it very clear how he felt about me with other guys.

"The painting thing was a complete disaster. It's startlingly dull after the titillating episodes that came before it. And it sends an inconsistent message."

"And what is that?

"It rips the viewer off. After investing in eight episodes of sexy, edgy programming about a woman exploring her sexual preferences. What they're left with is someone doing everything she can to avoid intimacy in order to appease a jealous lover. A relationship contractually prohibited, by the way."

Yes, that pretty much summed it up.

"Which leaves the last one." The rolling of the pen between her palms stopped. "If the lead singer of the Dragons is going to be the culmination of your journey, your sexual ideal, then the viewers actually need to see it. To get the visual payoff. You and Marsha put your heads together. Script out your solutions and email them directly to me. If I find them satisfactory, we'll call the crew back in and get back to work."

"But maybe Lucky and the guys won't agree to redo those scenes with me."

"Oh, they will. Each one signed a contract much like yours. Mr. Morris and I have already taken care of the logistics. The band has an upcoming show in New Jersey. All the parties involved will remain here in the city afterward to film. They'll only lose a couple of days off. A small price to pay. For them. For Marsha. For you." She tapped her pen on her desk as if it were a gavel. "Rock Fuck Club is going to cement my reputation. It will make you a household name. Women exploring their sexual interests on their own terms without judgement. That's the original theme. That's the focus of the launch for the first season. That's the way the series will continue under my supervision, and that's the way I'll ensure that it ends. I won't accept anything less." She let go of her pen. It rolled to a stop on her desk. "You screwed up, Miss Winters, but I'm going to fix it. We're going to do more than just salvage Rock Fuck Club. We're going to make it a huge success."

I STEPPED OUTSIDE WMO in a daze. Beneath the shadow of the huge building, I felt like I was right back where I had started, only with one notable difference. I now knew exactly what I stood to lose. Lucky. And everything we had found together. What Smith was proposing would put it all at extreme risk.

Kissing Rocky? Sexy aftercare with him? When I knew Lucky would handle it about as well as he had the initial scene? Which was to say…not well at all.

And Alec. The symbolic painting of the Dragon logo on my back by him and the rest of the band. It sounded like she wanted to scrap the whole thing. What in the hell could I come up with to replace it? What would be tantalizing enough to satisfy the exec, but yet tame enough to keep Lucky from hating me?

At least the last one, the abrupt scene before Lucky and I had taken off for Morris' penthouse, would be easy enough to sex up. If Lucky wasn't furious with the results of the other retakes.

"Hey." Marsha tapped my arm. "You ok?"

"Hardly." I gave it to her real. "But much better than I would've been if I had faced Suzanne Smith's wrath alone."

"You'll never be alone while I have any say in it." She grabbed my hand and squeezed it.

"Oops. Sorry. Hey." Barbara stepped out of the building and glanced back and forth between Marsha and me. "You two took off so quickly I didn't get a chance to give you your hotel information." She pointed over my shoulder. "I booked you a room at the Hilton Midtown. I would've booked two, but…"

"We're good with one."

"I imagine you are. You seem tight." She looked a little envious. "I had a close friend once, or at least I thought I did. In the end she was just being nice to me because she had a thing for my dad." My brows rose. That sounded awful. "But anyway, your friendship was what I found most engaging about your YouTube channel. It's sweet how you look out for each other."

"Yeah, we do," Marsha said. "And we used to be a lot more fun before your boss came into the picture."

"Suzanne can be severe at times." Barbara glanced over her shoulder as if she feared Smith would throw open the glass door and berate her.

"So Barbara," Marsha said to regain the assistant's attention. "Is there a good bar at our hotel?"

"I think it closes at nine." Barbara tucked a lose strand of her hair behind her ear.

"What kind of bar closes at nine?"

"Ones in Midtown. Most of the workers have already gone home for the day by then. It gets deserted down here around now."

"You sound like you know from personal experience."

She nodded.

"She works you late a lot, huh?'"

"Yes. But the pay's good. And it's a foot in the door inside a field that interests me."

"How's that?" I asked, remembering Smith's words earlier.

"Music production involves a lot of the same skill sets I use here. I don't play an instrument or sing, but I've been told I have a good ear. I'd like to discover new acts. Help in the recording studio. Maybe have a label of my own one day."

"That sounds really cool," I looked at her in a new light. With her professional demeanor softened as it was now she seemed younger, more like a contemporary and less like a Suzanne Smith clone.

"Know any place close that's still open?" Marsha queried. "Someplace you can come with us so we can get to know each other better? Preferably with alcohol? Someplace we can have some fun?"

"YOU SURE YOU'RE up for this bestie?" Marsha peered at me skeptically. "The last rider who got thrown didn't look so good." She hooked a thumb over the chest high wall that corralled a mechanical bull and padding of dubious quality. A bucket even stood by at the ready in case someone needed to hurl.

Um, no. I wasn't sure. But I wouldn't admit it. I still remembered how to have fun. We'd done some shots. Now it was time to cinch up my wild and crazy belt a notch. A little Manhattan mayhem Texas style.

"I can do this," I confirmed, trying not to lose my nerve as I watched a staff member in a Johnny Utah t-shirt usher off the second guy in a row who had face planted on the mat after only a three second ride. "I'm no tenderfoot, Mars. Let me show 'em how it's done."

"You're hard core, girl. But I wouldn't do it if I were you." She shook her head as they opened the gate beside us and let in the next person in line.

"Might as well. I've already signed the release forms. Besides, I need something to do besides worry about a situation that has no easy solution."

"True. I'm all for ill-advised distractions. But wouldn't it be better if we just went back to the bar with our new friend Barbara?" She winced as the most recent rider slash victim landed on the padding only inches away from us. "Safer?" she added wryly.

"Since when did you or I ever go the safe route?"

"Since never." She grinned and dropped her gaze to the woman in the rhinestone encrusted cowboy boots who was currently crawling away from the victorious bull. "How was it?"

"My girlfriends convinced me they would go easier on a woman."

"They're never easier on the women, honey." Mars shook her head and pointed at the control booth. "That guy over there's getting his kicks outta using that mechanical demon to make us look stupid."

"You're probably right," she muttered, straightening her hat. "Makes me want to try it again just to spite him." She started to spin around to go back, but the gate attendant grabbed her by the shoulders.

"Uh-uh. One ride per night, Calamity Jane."

"Fine." Calamity wobbled toward the gate, then stopped in front of us. "You next?" she asked Marsha.

"Nope." She hooked a thumb at me.

"Well good luck to you, sister. My advice? Approach it like the rest of rough things that come at us in this life. Stay loose in the saddle. Go with the ride. But whatever you do, hold on tight to those reins."

"THAT'S THE THIRD time he's tried to get a hold of you, honey." Marsha put her hand on my shoulder, or at least I think it was hers. It could have belonged to one of the guys who kept coming over to the bar and hitting on me. There had been more than a few since we had entered the below the street level honky-tonk themed bar.

"I can't talk to him yet, Mars." My words were muffled into my arms. I had them crossed on the bar and my face pressed into them. We still hadn't come up with a solution. We'd been full of grandiose ambitions before the shots, but I was so plastered now I couldn't even hold my head up without the room spinning. "I'm too wasted to deflect. He's gonna hate me when he finds out what I have to do. He should hate me. I'm too much trouble. He should choose easy. Take what those groupies are offering."

"You know he's not interested in that scene. He's in love with you, Raven. He's gonna be mad, sure. Every relationship comes with its share of troubles. But he's gonna be more understanding if you level with him upfront."

"He'll hate me if I tell him now. He'll hate me if I won't. What's the difference?"

"The difference is you wouldn't be keeping it from him. You're building trust. It's better that you break it to him yourself before his record label does."

Her cell rang. Not mine for a change. Hallelujah. Maybe Lucky had given up for the night and gone to bed.

"Hello." Marsha's voice sounded far away like she was at the end of a long tunnel. "Yeah, Lucky. She's sitting right beside me, but she can't talk. She's totally trashed."

"Mars, don't tell hm tht." I tried to lift my head, but only ended up bumping my chin on the bar. It was wise that Barbara had already gotten into a taxi and headed home for the night. I was way past the point of being fun.

"I'm putting her on speaker. You're gonna need me to translate. She's slurring her consonants, a sure sign that the light's about to go out."

"Raven," Lucky said my name in his I'm-the-boss-of-the-tour voice. F. U. C. K. My spine tried to snap straight, but it only managed a weak quiver. Absent my usual sass, there was only longing. Plus, a big dose of regret that I was pulling him into my drama yet again. "Marsha, is she still there?"

"She's here. Barely. Her eyes are open, but they're glazed like a Krispy Kreme."

"What's going on, Angel? Why are you avoiding my calls? And why in the bloody hell are you getting pissed in public? Wherever you are please tell me Marsha isn't recording you."

"Hey frontman. Marsha here. I resent that last remark. I told you I would look out for her and keep her off the grid. And I have. Mostly. You're girl's a little strong-willed. I tried to talk her out of riding the mechanical bull. But she thought she had something to prove. And I wouldn't doubt that some guys might've filmed her. Not because they recognized her, but because maybe they were imagining her riding them instead of the bull."

"Bloody hell!" he exclaimed. "Marsha you're bollucks as a bodyguard. She would've been safer with Sky as her chaperone."

CHAPTER
Ten

"STAY WITH ME, BESTIE." Marsha somehow got me through the hotel lobby and into the elevator. I had surfaced a bit from my alcohol induced stupor during the cab ride from the club. The lights of Times Square shining on the back of my eyelids like the sun had dissipated some of my tequila fog. But by the time we checked in at the Hilton things were blurring in and out again. "Don't you dare puke in here." She put her palm on my sternum and propped me up against the wall of the elevator when I started to list forward. "The guy at the front desk reminded me three times if you toss it anywhere they're gonna charge my credit card a five hundred dollar clean up fee."

"But..." My eyes going wide, I put a hand over my mouth and felt my ears pop and my stomach drop precipitously as I watched the numbers on the elevator panel rocketing higher.

"Thirty-three," Marsha announced way too cheerily and took my arm. "C'mon."

"Slow down," I warned her as she linked her arm with mine

and half-dragged me down the hall. "The floor is wavy." I swallowed repeatedly. The odds were about fifty-fifty right now on that cleaning fee.

"It's not, but don't worry. We're at our room."

"Yay," I said weakly, leaning my shoulder into the wall beside the door." My vision wouldn't clear. I squinted to focus but that only narrowed my foggy field of vision. She fed a card into the reader. It whirred and clicked. "Here we go, honey." Marsha took my arm again and helped me inside the room. A whoosh of musty air hit me as the door closed behind us. Spotting the bathroom on the left, I immediately veered into it and dropped to my knees in front of the toilet. My bestie joined me just in time to pull my hair out of the way. Heave after heave, I rejected the excess tequila. She stayed through several wracking bouts, stroking my spine soothingly between eruptions.

"I screwed up," I told her, taking the hand towel she offered and wiping my mouth. "So sorry I got sick on you."

"It's ok, baby," she soothed. "I'm here for better or worse." Marsha left me briefly at some point, but she didn't abandon me. She returned and set a chilled bottled water beside me, a pillow and a blanket. But I wasn't able to make use of any of it for a long while.

Yeah, it was that bad.

When it was finally over, my stomach was so sore it felt like someone had kicked me in it. My reward for my stupidity. That plus my dry mouth and a pounding headache. Not to mention the bruises along my inner thighs from the bull. I made a note to myself, hoping I would heed it the next time I was tempted to escape my problems with alcohol.

One shot with my bestie and zero mechanical bulls.

I rose slowly and grabbed the edge of the cold counter to steady myself. I filled a glass with tap water and took the Tylenol Marsha had left for me. I avoided my reflection. I didn't need to make this any worse than it already was.

After carefully stripping off my clothes, I took a long shower and washed my hair. I felt more like myself by the time I was done. Wrapping a big white towel around me, I stepped out. My comb and a toothbrush were on the counter near where the pain reliever had been, within easy reach. Again, my bestie had anticipated and set out exactly what I would need. When I was done rinsing with the complimentary hotel mouthwash, I gripped the counter again and lifted my gaze to face the reflection I had been avoiding.

"Oh my." I put a hand to my rounded mouth. The woman who stared back at me with her long dark hair dripping into the white towel looked like a wraith. My skin was paler than usual. My golden eyes had purple smudges beneath them. My cheekbones seemed hollow and my lips were chapped.

"No more benders," I told my reflection. "You're too smart to act this stupid." Hearing a ping from my phone, I turned and noticed Marsha had placed it on a folded washcloth on the floor, screen side up. I knelt down carefully and scooped it up.

Marsha: I heard the shower. How r u feeling?

Raven: Like hell. Is Dr. West in? I could really use some wise counsel.

Marsha: i dont know about wisdom but i luv u & want what's best for u. Will that work?

Raven: Yeah, for sure.

I set the phone down on the counter, took my towel off and replaced it with Lucky's Killers t-shirt. Yes, Marsha had set out a change of clothes, too. Longing pierced the left side of my chest as the soft cotton settled around my shoulders. I lifted the edge of the collar to my nose. Mandarin and rum, his scent still lingered on it.

"Hey." I shuffled out of the bathroom and into the bedroom. Her face aglow from her phone's display, Marsha set it down on the mattress and pulled herself up into a seated position on the bed.

"You look terrible."

"I know. Thanks for taking care of me." I would have shrugged a shoulder, but my tummy was feeling too iffy for unnecessary movement.

"I only did what you would do for me. Sit here beside me." She threw back the covers and scooted over on the bed leaving a space for me.

"Most unconventional therapist ever. Booze and booty calls," I quipped lamely, climbing in beside her.

"What do you expect? I don't even have a license." She flipped the covers over my legs. "But for some reason you keep coming back. I must be doing something right." Smiling softly, she tucked the blankets tighter around my lap. "You should've used the blow dryer on your hair. You're going to be cold with your hair all wet, and you always get the frizzies when you air dry."

"Who's to see?" I shrugged, and my stomach reminded me why that was a bad idea.

"Hmm. He might not be here, bestie." Her brows creased together. "But you still need to take care of yourself. I'm in enough trouble with your man as it is. He's gonna kick my ass about tonight. I put a ginger ale on the nightstand. Why don't you try to sip on it? If we get you rehydrated maybe you'll start to feel better sooner."

"I will." I slowly twisted, picked up the can and took a careful sip using the straw. "I love you, Mars," I said after I was sure the liquid was going to stay down.

"I love you, too. It's pretty sad that you have a bestie so well versed in how to treat a hangover." She patted my leg. "So take another sip and then talk to me. I wanna know why you're so emotional. It's not like you to overdo it with the booze. And before that with Smith? You practically caved into every one of her stipulations."

"She holds all the cards this time," I grumbled.

"Um no, she doesn't. She left a couple of aces. One, her reputation is on the line. Two, she expects this show to be huge. She wants it to be. She *needs* it to be. We can use that to our advantage. Plus, I'm pretty sure Barbara would help us if we ask. But Smith and her PA aside, something's changed. I know you. I know the way you are. Tonight was very unlike you. What's going on? What's happened since we last talked?"

"I got a little scuffed up by a stampede of Lucky's fans in Atlanta. He made a unilateral decision and kicked me off the tour until he can work out a scenario that is quote safe for me unquote. He doesn't trust me to take care of myself. And what I did tonight sure didn't help." My stomach roiled anew.

"Wow." She shook her head. "How scuffed up are we talking about?"

"Some road rash on my palms from the concrete when I fell. An inch-long gash on my knee."

"That must have been scary."

"It was. But it's nothing compared to how bad I feel now. I love him, Mars, and I trust him. But between you and me, we both know how things are on the road. With Ivan, I ignored a lot of the warning signs. I can't do that with Lucky. I won't do that with him. I want him, all of him, all to myself."

"Did you tell him that?" She whispered.

"Yeah, basically." I nodded.

"What did he say?"

"After he got mad for me questioning his integrity?"

"Oh, honey." She shook her head sadly.

I sighed. "He took me to the airport. He told me to do whatever it took to make Smith happy. That he would work on the security problems on his end. That he wants us to be together."

"You've got some situational stress on your relationship for sure. And I certainly get now why you acted the way you did with Smith. But if you give WMO all they want they're gonna have you do stuff that's gonna make an alpha male like Lucky go insane."

"Yeah, I know. I guess that's why I overdid it tonight. To escape my problems, but they're still there. It was dumb."

"We all do stupid stuff, Raven. He's not going to hold that against you." She was probably right about the night's alcohol binge. But it was the other stuff that worried me. My current predicament with the executive was the top priority to sort out. Caving might get me out of her clutches the fastest. But capitulating might also cost me Lucky. I had to think this through carefully. I had to find a solution that worked for the short and the long term. The long term being my relationship with my favorite sexy frontman.

BY THE MORNING I had reached a decision. I paced the length of our hotel room working out the logistics in my mind while Marsha went to get us some decent coffee. The caffeine was mostly an excuse. I knew she needed a sanity break from my emotional state. I stopped pacing to look out the window. Cars and taxis filled the Avenue of the Americas below, typical early morning traffic in Manhattan. The sky was too cloudy to see where the rising sun was in the sky, but I knew it was too early to call Lucky.

My cell started ringing. I scooped it off the bed and glanced at the display. It was my dad. We had been conversing regularly since our reconciliation. "Hey Daddy," I answered. "How are you? Is everything ok?"

"Hi, Raven. Yes, it is. Only it's hot as Hades down here. My drum major passed out during marching practice and almost toppled from his platform, but we got him hydrated and everything turned out fine in the end."

"Oh, well that's good." I took another sip of my soda. I needed to replenish my fluids, too.

"Are you drinking enough water out there?" I queried. He was a lot older than his students.

"I carry a camel pack with me at all times, but thanks for looking out for me. Miss you, Raven. How are you? I tried to get a hold of you yesterday. I called Lucky, and he told me you were in New York. Is everything ok between you two?"

I shook my head, tears choking my reply.

"Raven, are you still there?" he prompted.

"Yeah, Daddy. It's just that things are a little strained with Lucky right now." The words started tumbling out. "WMO is putting pressure on me. Lucky and the Dragons are a real hot commodity because of the success of their new single. His fans are getting too pushy, and he thinks it might be best if I'm away from the tour until he can improve the security situation."

"But you want to be with him regardless of the risk."

"Yes." That was it exactly.

"I understand his point of view. He wants you safe, darling. I want that, too. But I also understand your side. Being separated when you're in love is difficult. Your mom never wanted us to be apart, either."

"Yeah?" I dropped to the bed. I loved to hear anything he would share about my mom. Sure it made me miss her more to talk about her. But sharing our memories drew my father and me closer.

Be brave, I could almost hear her say. I reached for the pendant that had been my mother's wedding ring. It hung from my neck on my brother's chain. A part of her and a part of him. Both gone now, I closed my fingers around the tangible reminder of them.

"She left all she knew behind when she came with me to Dallas. I don't think we were ever apart more than a few days. Even after you and your brother were born, she refused to pursue a musical career of her own. It's hard to be separated from someone who's your best friend and your better half."

"It is." I thought about that. Marsha held the title of best friend, but Lucky filled that role as well. In different ways. It wasn't an either or situation. I needed them both. And was he my better half? I knew that answer immediately. Hell, yes.

"So what are you going to do about it?" My father asked gently. "The pressure WMO is putting on you? And the rest?"

"I'm going to do the best I can do. For WMO. For Lucky. For all the people I love. For myself."

"That's my girl." He was quiet a long moment. I was, too, as I absorbed his praise. "That's exactly how your mom would've tackled it."

"I know. Thanks, Dad. I just hope I can pull it off."

"Do you remember the stories she used to tell you about the Navajo monsters?"

"Yeah."

"The *Yeetso* was your favorite."

"He's the biggest one."

"Yes. Do you remember how you're supposed to weaken or slay a monster?"

"You have to learn all you can about its destructive powers so you can understand what it can potentially do to you and what you can do to it. Knowledge is the key to defeating or destroying it."

"Do you have the knowledge that you need, daughter?"

"Yes, Daddy." I thought of the things Marsha had pointed out about Suzanne Smith. This time I needed to make the exec believe she needed me more than I needed her. "That's just what I needed to hear. I'm glad you called."

"I'm glad I did, too. I want you to come visit me for Christmas. Bring Lucky. Marsha, too. All your new friends. Would you consider doing that?"

"Yes." I smiled. "I'd love to."

"Angel." Lucky answered his phone on the first ring. My heart fluttered, and my eyes filled, but I blinked back the tears and willed my pulse to slow. If I wanted to have any prayer of keeping Lucky and protecting what we had found together I was going to have to stop feeling sorry for myself and start taking some proactive steps to deal with my dilemma. "Are you ok? I tried to call you after the bar, but Marsha said you were ill."

"Yeah. I was up most of the night. I acted stupid because I was scared."

"I don't want you to be frightened, Raven. I told you we'll work this out."

"I know you did, Lucky, and we will. But you need to remember I'm the other half of the equation. You're going to have to let me contribute to a solution. Suzanne Smith had Marsha and me in her office last night. She made some threats about breach of contract. She's demanding some changes in the filming of my season."

"What threats? What changes?"

"Monetary penalties. She wants to reshoot some of the footage involving Rocky, Alec and you. She's already gotten Morris involved. He's going to have the band stay in New York for a couple of days after your show in Jersey. Basically, I think it's going to come down to me giving Suzanne the sex appeal she's seeking, which I'm willing to do, but my own way. I need to be true to myself and why I started the Rock Fuck Club in the first place. I want to run my ideas by you before I go to her with them. We're a team now. And I want our team to grow stronger. We have to be stronger. There are a lot of forces out there that could tear us apart if we let them."

I held my breath, wanting him to reassure me.

"Angel, I would do anything for you. But…"

"But what?" I really needed to hear absolutes from him, confirmation that there wasn't anything in the world that could come between us.

"But I've seen how sexy you can be. And I prefer that any new experimentation along those lines be between you and me without any cameras around. With that being said, I love you, and I love that you thought to come to me first. So why don't you tell me what you have in mind."

CHAPTER
eleven

"**H**AVE YOU HEARD FROM SMITH YET?" Marsha asked from her seat on the bench beside me.

"No." I swiveled away from the distant view of the Statue of Liberty out the boat window behind us to face her instead. "I checked my cell before we pulled away from the dock."

"Damn." A briny wind whipped a streamer of her blonde hair across her pretty face. The wind was strong today. It was snapping the flags on top of the Staten Island Ferry as we had boarded it.

"Yeah, she's taking her sweet time to mull it over. But I know what she's doing. It's an old negotiating technique." I had looked up a bunch of stuff on the internet after talking to my dad. Business articles about tactics. What to say, what not to. I was going to be better prepared the next time the WMO exec and I met. "Even if she gets back to me today, I'm not returning communication until tomorrow. Let her squirm for a while. It's her turn to be in the hot seat. Right?"

"Welcome back, badass bestie." Marsha took my hand, looked

in my eyes and smiled encouragingly. The PA system crackled to life giving instructions on disembarkation. When the announcement was through, Marsha's expression returned to reflective lines. "What did Lucky say when you told him your plan and everything?"

"He was cautiously supportive." I shrugged. Mostly, he had postponed further discussion until we could talk in person. He wasn't happy. I could hear it in his voice. I wasn't happy, either. Making the best we could of a bad situation sucked. Worry over the outcome of that upcoming conversation with him made the tortured post-bender lining of my stomach churn. Truthfully, it had started the moment I had woken up. Anxiety had dampened my enthusiasm all day. Grand Central Station, Rockefeller Center, Central Park and now the Staten Island ferry, the highlights of New York tour should have been fun except instead of feeling like a mirthless marathon. I had pasted on a smile for all the photos and videos Marsha took. It had been nice the two of us hanging out like old times, but my glued on grin was starting to loosen. Not that my bestie was fooled.

"It'll be ok." She squeezed my captured hand again.

"It will, or it won't." I withdrew my hand and swiveled away, gazing back to the water. But I wasn't focused on the setting sun, the seagulls flying overhead or any of the few other watercraft in the distance. I mentally replayed the images I had sorted through on the Dragons' Facebook page. Lucky was so sexy in them, but he wasn't ever alone. No, of course not. Sure, it was mostly him at meet and greets. Lots of times it had been me taking the commemorative cellphone shots for the fans. But when I had been there it hadn't seemed as though he had held the girls as close or allowed them to be so bold with him. I hadn't felt threatened by them then the way I was feeling now.

So many girls. Too many with their hands on the center of his naked chest or low on his abdomen. Apparently while I'd been dosing my anxiety with tequila shots, he had been doing his fair share of self-medicating, too. A Captain Morgan's rum bottle dangled from his fingertips in many of the more recent photos. I had a pretty good idea why he was wearing sunglasses in them and why his response to what I had revealed about WMO had been so strangely muted.

Not that he doesn't care, I reminded myself. He had only been hung over. We both had been suffering the unpleasant aftereffects of hitting the liquor too hard.

The evidence, should he choose to examine it, was right there in front of him. Being separated wasn't good for us. Errors in judgment happened when alcohol gets involved. Mistakes could be forgiven like Marsha had said, but only if they didn't go too far. We needed each other. Day by day. Night by night. We were better and stronger side by side.

We disembarked, took the escalator downstairs and had just hit the sidewalk when my cell started ringing.

"Hello," I answered, unable to see the display in the glare.

"Hi, Raven."

"Oh hey, Barbara." I recognized the voice. "Thanks for returning my call." Beside me, Marsha raised a brow and shifted in closer. We were an island of two in a steady stream of flowing foot traffic.

"No problem. I usually take a break around dinner time. Where are you?"

"Battery Park."

"During rush hour? I bet it's crazy with tourists and locals."

"Yeah, it's like the freeways back home in Dallas with more people instead of cars." I got bumped suddenly and nearly dropped my phone. "Hey, I was wondering if we might get together and chat somewhere. I have some questions for you about WMO and your boss that I hope you might be willing to answer."

"What kind of questions?"

"Basic stuff really. She credits you for getting her interested in the RFC project. I wanted to hear more about that. Get a better understanding of what she wants from me. That kind of thing."

"Oh yeah, sure. She's actually been in meetings all day related to Rock Fuck Club."

Interesting, I thought. No doubt she had read my emailed proposal. Already, I was getting useful information from Barbara. My dad's advice had been sound. Smith might not be a mythological monster, but she definitely wasn't my buddy. Best to get all the information I could about her.

MARSHA AND I were sitting across a picnic table from each other with cups of beer and burgers in plastic baskets when Barbara arrived. I froze with a French fry slathered in ketchup halfway to my mouth. Not because Barbara looked out of place in the casual burger joint in her high end business suit and classy heels but because of who was with her.

"What's wrong?" Marsha swiveled around in her seat to follow the direction of my gaze.

"Holy shit!" she exclaimed amid the murmurs of recognition that rose as Barbara and her escort both moved toward our table. The ketchup drip, drip, dripped onto the wax paper before I finally unthawed myself from my shock and dropped the forgotten fry. I was just wiping off my hands with a napkin when they reached us.

"Hi." I rose and stepped over the bench to greet them.

"Hey, baby." Rayne Michaels, the handsome lead singer of Sundown and coincidently Rock Fuck Club fuck number one leaned closer and pressed a kiss that lingered too long on my cheek.

"Dad's in town for a concert." Barbara wasn't frowning, but I noted definite brackets of tight lipped displeasure around her mouth. "He insisted on coming with me when he found out I was meeting you."

"You look beautiful, Raven." Rayne flashed his megawatt rock star grin. If he had been on stage the bras and panties would have been flying through the air and landing at his feet. "Mind if I sit with you while you and my daughter talk business?"

His daughter. Barbara *Michaels.* I saw the resemblance now. The same sandy blonde hair. The same green eyes. A very uncommon shade, like weathered sea-glass.

"I do mind, actually." I hitched my chin up.

"Raven." Marsha hissed giving me a sharp look. But I didn't want to play nice with Rayne. Besides, the fact that his appearance had shaken me, all around us people were snapping pictures with their cells. Who knew where those photos would end up being posted, and who might potentially see and be hurt by them. I certainly didn't need any more drama in my life.

"No. It's alright." The lead singer spread a cocky grin almost as lethal as Lucky's. "I caught you off guard. I should have called first. I'll go sit at the bar. Get a drink. Maybe when you're through talking with Barb, we can catch up. Sound good?"

"Maybe," I replied noncommittally. I would have said no outright except that Marsha was staring me down giving me the nonverbal cue to be diplomatic. As he sauntered off, she tipped back on her bench to watch. "That man has a fine ass," she decided before she returned her attention to the table. "Oh, sorry, Barbara." She grimaced.

"It's ok. I'm used to it." Used to it she might be, but it certainly didn't make her happy. I frowned. This might be harder than I anticipated, getting her to open up to me.

"Would you like something to eat?" I asked her, noticing her longing look at my burger.

"Yeah. Only I'm on a diet. Again." She sighed.

"Their veggie burgers look pretty good."

"That sounds great. I didn't get a chance to eat all day. Sergeant, I mean Suzanne wouldn't let me leave my desk."

"I'll put the order in." Marsha patted the PA's delicate hand where it rested on the table. "How about a light beer to go with it? If you didn't eat all day, I bet you can afford the extra calories."

"I can. Thank you."

"No problem. I'll be right back."

"Wait," Barbara said as Marsha stood. "Let me give you my credit card." She started digging around inside the purse she had on her lap. A large leather purse, it was almost as big as my traveling duffle. Old and worn, incongruent with her elegant attire.

"Our treat," I insisted. "We invited you to dinner."

"Alright." She nodded and Marsha headed to the bar, taking a long circuitous route that had her passing by Rayne and the crowd that had already gravitated around the superstar. I turned back to Barbara wondering how to begin. She was still combing through the items in her monstrous bag. She withdrew a pair of reading glasses, slid them on and pulled out her cell which she set on the table.

"It's my nana's purse," she explained, noting my interest. "We were close. She's gone now, but she used to always fill it with candy. I called her the Candy Nana. It still smells like her peppermints. Suzanne hates that I still carry the thing." She covered her mouth like she hadn't meant to let that last part slip.

"Suzanne is pretty hard-ass."

Paling, Barbara nodded.

"She's making my life pretty damn miserable," I admitted finding myself warming to the girl who seemed less reserved outside the walls of WMO.

"Veggie burger. All the condiments," Marsha returned. "Cheese on the side." She set a plastic cup full of beer beside the basket of food.

"Thanks." Barbara took a napkin from the dispenser on the table, placed it in her lap and dug in. Marsha and I finished our fries while the PA ate her burger and its toppings like a salad. She cut each bite into equal sized pieces. She and Alec would be instant soul mates and drive Cody crazy. I felt a sharp pang of longing for the family I had been forced to leave behind.

"Was my...fling with your dad how you found out about RFC?" I asked Barbara when her food was finished. Refocusing on the task at hand, I needed to find a way to turn the situation at WMO to my advantage.

She nodded, putting down her fork and taking another sip of her beer. "He fell for you, you know." She glanced over at her dad in case it didn't register who she was referring to. Rayne was watching us. He lifted his chin.

"He falls for all the women he sleeps with. He justifies it in his mind that way. It's what he used to tell my mother when they were married."

"Oh. I'm sorry. That must have been..."

"Weird. Humiliating. Pointless. My mother enabled him too long. All they did was argue and cut at each other by the end. She's still in counseling."

"Love isn't always easy, and it doesn't always have happy endings." I met Barbara's gaze, speaking to myself as much as to her. But I could also see in the PA's darkened eyes how much her parents' situation had affected her. I touched her hand. Empathy rose within me. "My mother's gone. My dad and I took it real hard. But even though it still hurts, we cherish the time we had with her." Eyes bright, I glanced at Marsha. She glanced away. She didn't want to talk about my brother or about the fact that she settled for meaningless hookups when she deserved so much more. "Love is hard," I continued my voice thick. "Love has risks. Sometimes it gets taken away too soon, and sometimes you get hurt many times before you find the person who's right for you." Like with Ivan and me. "But when you find the right one, you sacrifice, you hold on, you fight for what you have and you do everything you can to keep it."

"You and Lucky seem like a good match. I can see doing everything you can for a guy like him. But in my experience those types of guys are few and far between." She looked down at my hand on hers and then glanced up speculatively. "I'm sorry for sounding so pessimistic." She put her hand over mine, sandwiching our fingers together and studying me for a long beat. "So Lucky Spencer? Worth holding onto? Worth fighting for? Worth keeping?"

"Yes. Absolutely," I answered firmly.

"I figured so. I've seen all the episodes several times. For my job of course. Even the footage with the two of you that we didn't use seems to point to you guys being solid."

"We're a couple now. I'm trying to keep what we have..." I trailed off, swallowed hard. "I can't let the things your boss wants me to do tear us apart. What happened with Ivan...if it had been Lucky who had cheated on me...I wouldn't have ranted and raved and started Rock Fuck Club. It would have ruined me."

"I guess there are differing degrees of attachment." She cocked her head to the side, a tendril of her blonde hair sliding free from her chignon. "It sounds like you and Lucky have a seriously special bond."

"I believe we do." It was time to put all my cards on the table. "I like you Barbara Michaels."

"I like you, too, Raven Winters."

I smiled. "I don't want to get you into get any trouble, but if you know anything that might help me, I would appreciate your telling me. I sent a proposal to your boss..."

"Yeah, I read it. Suzanne went ballistic. Not because it's a bad plan. Mostly because she's used to people bowing down before her."

"Truly?" I cringed.

"Stick to your guns. Your plan will work. It's the truth. *Your* truth. The cameras will pick up on that. And I think when she cools down she'll realize how sexy your truth is."

"Even the parts with Alec and Cody?"

"Yes. Don't let her tell you how to write your story. Love is love, right? It's as different and unique as we all are as individuals. Sergeant Smith would remake you into her own image if you let her. Like she's been trying to do to me since I've been working for her." Barbara sat up straighter in her chair. "Produce the ending you proposed. I want to see that. Lots of people will." She leaned forward and curled her finger beckoning Marsha to lean in, too. "I'll let you in on a secret. The viewing of the series by our target demographic all the way up until the encounter with Rocky are fantastic. That's why Smith wants to redo the rest. And she senses how big this could be. She wants additional material, too. Behind the scenes footage. Background interviews with you and your hookups. She even has me scouting right now for a second season star." She shifted her gaze to Marsha for a tellingly long moment before returning her attention fully to me "Bargain with her, Raven. You just might get everything you want, or at least what you need to hold onto Lucky."

CHAPTER
Twelve

"**R**AVEN!"
I bolted out of deep sleep, blinking to gain my bearings as I registered that the pounding I had heard in my dream was really on the door to my hotel room.

"Open the door, Angel or I'm busting the bloody thing off its hinges!"

"Lucky!" I gasped. Throwing the covers back, I leapt from my bed at the same time the lamp next to it switched on.

"It's four in the morning," Marsha grumbled. "I thought he was getting here this evening, and that we were meeting him at the club in Jersey." Sitting up in her bed, her blonde hair snarled around her face, my bestie seemed less discombobulated than I was. I wondered if she was still having trouble sleeping. "Does this ever stop? The circus that is your life?"

"Apparently not," I answered on the way to the door thinking that she would have to get used to the rodeo if she got roped into being the season two star of Rock Fuck Club. Flicking the safety latch aside, I unbolted the lock and threw open the door.

"About fucking time." Lucky swept a quick narrow eyed glance over me before he stormed inside the room. His helmet clamped in the crook of his arm, his expression was thundercloud dark. He went directly to the bathroom searching the interior of it, even throwing back the shower curtain before he exited then scanned the rest of the room as if expecting to find someone else besides Marsha and me within it.

"It's just us," I stated the obvious carefully as he spun back around to face me.

"Of course it is." He raked a hand through his inky hair. His expression softened as he trailed his gaze over me. "So that's where my favorite shirt went." I had worn the Killers tee to bed. I had packed it and taken it with me, though I hadn't exactly gotten his permission.

"Hey, Lucky." Marsha waved at him drawing his attention to her. "Don't mind me." Grinning, my bestie tossed her rumpled covers aside. "I'll just go into the bathroom for a while. Turn on the water. Have a nice long shower. The water pipes are really loud. I won't hear a thing while y'all work this out." She started to step around Lucky.

"Wait. Actually, you can have this." He set his helmet on the dresser and then reached into the front pocket of his jeans to pull out a paper sleeve with the Hilton logo on it. "Here. It's for the room across the hall." Looking perplexed, Marsha took the key from his outstretched hand. "I wasn't exactly sure of my reception," he explained. "I got an extra room just in case."

"Alright." Marsha turned to me. "But it's up to my bestie to decide if she wants me to stay or go."

"It's ok, Mars." I held her gaze, but I could feel Lucky's on me.

"Then I'll go." She nodded once at me, but shook the card at

Lucky. "You owe me big for pulling a stunt like this in the middle of the night, mister." She moved toward the door, lifting the key up in the air over her head. "I'll be across the hall if you need me, Raven."

"Angel." Lucky said, his voice a low tremble inducing rumble. He stepped closer to me before the door even closed behind Marsha. "It feels like forever since I last touched you." He reached for me, his hands closing firmly around my upper arms as he hauled me into him. I sagged into his strength, his solid foundation. His metal rings were hard, cold against my skin, but his fiercely possessive expression as he stared down at me softened and warmed me.

"Lucky, I missed you." A needful shudder rolling through me, I lifted my arms and draped them around his neck, tangling my fingers in his silky hair.

"Everything's wrong without you by my side." His grip flexed deeper into my flesh. "You understand that, don't you, Angel?" His stared down at me, his eyes intense pools of aquatic blue I immersed myself in.

"Yes I do." I untangled my fingers from his hair. "Because I feel the same way." I smoothed my hands along the line of his wide shoulders. "I need you, Lucky." I clawed at his shirt, desperate to get it out of the way in order to touch the warm skin beneath it. "I need you right now inside me. I need you to make everything right."

"There's my girl." His lips curling into a dark grin, he lowered his head. My thoughts scattered as he pressed his mouth to mine. His hands moved to my back. He slid them along the length of my spine. Aligning our bodies, he deepened the kiss. He slipped his wet tongue between my lips. Reaching my ass, he lifted each rounded globe in his firm grip. He centered me on his rock hard cock. He thrust his tongue deep into my mouth. I moaned and sucked on it while my hands dipped under the hem of his shirt and glided all over his smooth skin.

Gripping my ass tighter, he rocked me on his thick length and showed me with relentless strokes of his tongue and the bruising pressure of his lips how much he missed me.

"Lucky." I ripped my mouth from his and sucked in a breath of needed air as my knees went wobbly beneath me.

"I've got you, Angel." He lifted me completely off the ground. "Wrap your legs around me." As I complied, he quickly walked us backward to the bed. "This needs to go." Holding me with only one arm, he grabbed the hem of my borrowed shirt and whipped it over my head with the other. Nothing but me and my thong now remained. His gaze glowed as he took me in. My tits tightened beneath his regard. He growled and gripped my ass again with both his hands. Grabbing each cheek, he squeezed hard. His ringed fingers bit into my flesh. It stung. But wet heat erupted between my legs. It turned me on to know I made him so aroused. I grabbed fistfuls of his silky hair. He lowered his head and he kissed me again making me even hotter for him before he tore his lips from mine.

"Why…"

"Thong off, Raven." He lowered me. Feeling boneless, I slid my melted body along the turgid length of his. "Get in that bed right now," he ordered as my feet touched the carpet. "Get ready for me, babe. I've had a hard-on for you since I got on the Ducati and started imagining you just like this." His eyes a blue blaze, he reached over his shoulders, drew his shirt off and threw it aside. I stared at him and his chiseled chest. My lips parted. His curved upward. "Now, Angel." His sexy accent gave me another warm flesh tingling shiver. "Hurry."

"Ok." I quickly wiggled out of the lacy thong while he leaned against the dresser to remove his boots and socks. He didn't take his eyes off of me. My gaze certainly didn't stray as he unbuckled his belt and removed his jeans. My heart raced when he slid his boxers off and his engorged member sprang free. Mouth dry, I scrambled for the bed.

"Fuck, you're gorgeous." His gaze traveled the length of me as I lay on my back in the bed propped up on my elbows assuming a centerfold position with my knees bent and only slightly parted to give him a tantalizing peek.

"You are," I returned. Unashamed to be naked in front of him, my pussy throbbed in anticipation.

"You ready for me?" The mattress dipped as he came forward, put his weight on it and parted my legs.

"You know I am." I shuddered as he glided one of his warm hands along my thigh.

Straight like an arrow for my pussy he went, firmly swiping the pad of his thumb over my pulsing clit.

"So wet." Staring at me, he brought his glistening thumb to his mouth and sucked on it. "You taste ready."

"Hurry." I licked my dry lips.

"That's the plan." He plowed his hands under my ass, lifted me and positioned himself between my legs. Aligning his cock, he sank it inside me inch by steely hot inch until he was buried to the hilt. Then he circled his hips grinding all that delicious thick hardness into me.

"Oh, Lucky." I grabbed his tight ass, nearing orgasm just from the perfection of being filled with him. He pulled nearly all the way out and slowly sank inside me again. My scalp started to tingle. My bones turned molten. My muscles grew warm and languid and all that warm pleasure intensified as he swirled his hips.

"Wrap your legs tighter around me," he ordered gruffly, and I did, tightening every muscle in my body. I could feel the heavy pulse of him. He reached behind his back, grabbed my ankles and pressed them deeper into his ass. Balancing with his one hand on the mattress, he used it for leverage so he could plunge his hard cock deeper inside me.

"Oh, Lucky," I gasped and dug my heels into his ass on his next thrust.

"Yeah, baby. That's it. Take me." He groaned, his lids fluttering to half-closed. Returning both his hands to my ass, he gripped my skin hard enough to burn it and lifted me to bring me into his next deep thrust.

"Lucky, yes." That edge between pain and pleasure blurred. "Again. Harder. Please."

He grunted. He gave it to me harder. He gave it to me deeper. He gave it to me again and again and again. Every hot tingling sensation was centered on where we were joined. His hard to my soft. Then he got rough. He unlatched my crossed ankles. He grabbed my ass, and he started to hammer his cock into me. Wet and hot. Fast and deep. I took what he gave me. He was in control. He set the pace. It was brutal and beautiful. My breasts bounced. My nipples were hard. They ached. My skin burned. My muscles were locked so tight. I strained for it. I was so close. My entire body vibrated with the need for release.

He stiffened, and it came for me, a brilliant orgasm. It rolled through me like thunder and ripped me apart like a bolt of lightning. His release was just as violent. He threw back his head, roared my name and pumped his cock into me over and over again.

CHAPTER
Thirteen

WE SHOWERED SEPARATELY. Lucky first, then me, both of us pretending we weren't at an important juncture in our relationship when we both knew we were. We had to talk. The weight of what hadn't been said hung over this reunion like a heavy cloud.

Belting the complimentary hotel robe tight around my waist, I exited the bathroom. I needed a barrier. If there wasn't one in place, I knew my body would betray me. Lucky was lying in the bed. The one we had just made love in. His back propped against the headboard, he had his silky black boxers on. Apparently he needed a barrier of his own. His eyes followed me as I moved toward him.

"Lucky," I began, my voice rough as I leaned my hip into the bed beside him.

"Raven," he said at the same time. Smiling gently, he took my hand and settled it on his chest, at the center near his heart. As I stared down at where we were joined, a stray thought surfaced that made his beautiful gesture hurt. It reminded me of all of those other girls in the photos. I lifted my gaze to his blinking through the sting.

"You go first," I allowed. Stalling, I spread my fingers out to caress his smooth flesh.

"Angel, maybe you should. I had so many things I thought needed to be said, but now that I'm here with you, I've discovered that there's really only one." Tucking a finger under my chin, he lifted my head. His touch was all warmth. He had removed his metal rings. His gaze was warm, too, brilliant blindingly blue like the desert sky under a blazing sun. "I love you."

"I love you, too." Tears pooled in my eyes blurring the gorgeous vision of him. "And I don't want to lose you. I looked at the Facebook page the other day. I saw all those women putting their hands on you at the meet and greets. I didn't like it. It made me crazy. Probably cosmic payback for what you had to endure with me and the Rock Fuck Club. If I could take everything back, every single encounter from that time I would. I wish Rock Fuck Club had never happened."

"Then we would never have met," he said softly. "And you had things you had to figure out before you could be the woman you are right now. This stunning beautiful woman. The one who has completely captivated me. The one who has everything I need inside that unique heart of hers."

"You're everything I need, Lucky."

"I believe you, Raven. So no more looking back. The past is a stone we stepped on yesterday to get to the rock we're standing on together today." His gaze suddenly flashed remnant fire. "But I saw some photos that disturbed me, too. Can you please explain why you were with Rayne Michaels today? Why he touched you? Kissed you?"

"He did it before I could stop him. I didn't invite him to." His expression got scary hard, so I rushed to explain. "He's Barbara's father. Suzanne Smith's personal assistant. I had a meeting scheduled with her, and he tagged along. He touched my arm. He kissed my cheek in greeting. He was overly familiar, without a doubt. Maybe he imagines there's something between us. But there's nothing. I sent him away. I made him sit at the bar."

"That I would've liked to see. I'm sure a guy with an ego like his didn't fancy being dismissed. Why were you meeting with his daughter?"

"I was trying to gather information I could use as leverage with her boss. I'm tired of feeling like Suzanne has the upper hand. Tired of her manipulating me and pushing me around." I straightened my spine.

"Then she's done doing so." Lucky smiled encouragingly, trailing his warm fingers along my jaw, down my neck and sliding them across my chest as he spread the front of my robe open. My skin tingled everywhere he had touched me.

"Do you really think so?" My brows drew together. "She's pretty formidable. She's the youngest exec at WMO. She's accustomed to getting her way."

"What's driving her? Ambition? Greed? Something else?"

"I don't know." Maybe I should have talked to Barbara longer. I frowned.

"I don't think you necessarily need to know details, Raven. I was just trying to make the point that whatever her motivation is, ours is superior."

"And what is that?"

"Us." His brow dipped. "I'll admit I'm a dictator at times. You're used to running your own life. But from now on we're moving forward together as a team. We'll fight her for our sake, and when we fight together we'll win."

"That's exactly how I feel." My heavy heart lightened. "So you're ok with what I proposed? You didn't say much on the phone after I shared. I was unsure."

"I drank too much while you were gone. I was hung over. Being away from you was a lot harder than I anticipated."

"It's been horrible," I stated emphatically. "I hate it."

"We'll it's over now. For good." Grasping the edges of my robe, he glided it off my shoulders.

"Lucky," I began, only to lose my train of thought as he smoothed his warms hands over my breasts. My arms were trapped at my sides in the sleeves. My skin heated. My nipples drew to tight points. Lower, my pussy quivered. I surrendered to the sensations. My lids fluttered to half closed. My lips parted. I made a low keening sound.

"Yes, Raven. What do you need?" he asked, but he knew. My breath caught when he licked his fingers and painted my nipples wet.

"You remembered."

"I remember everything when it comes to you, Raven. Knowing what you like, what you need. It's important. I'm sorry I didn't pay proper attention in Atlanta. What happened there, when I saw you go down in the crowd and I couldn't get to you, it scared the bloody hell out of me."

"I'm sorry. I realize that. But nothing really serious happened." I arched my aching breasts into his worshipful hands. "Don't stop touching me. Please."

"But something could have." He lifted and shaped my breasts, tracing tighter and tighter circles around each, making the nipples pucker and me ache for more before he lifted his gaze.

"Nothing is likely to. Not if we're both careful." I moaned as he flicked the nipple with his thumb. "That feels so good." All of me thrummed with anticipation.

"I want you to stay with me and never leave because I'm weak where you're concerned, Raven, and entirely too selfish." He lifted me over his legs laying me out on the bed on the other side of him. Whipping his boxers off, he shifted and came up over me, his hand immediately gliding up my leg. "So you're going to have to promise to be cautious. Overly so." He parted the rest of my robe unwrapping me like I was a present and exposing all of me to his appreciative gaze. My arms remained trapped in the sleeves at my sides. My breasts heavy. My nipples taut. My clit throbbing. My pussy drenched. He skimmed his hand over it.

"I promise," I said breathily, lifting my hips into his caress.

"You would promise me anything right now." He sifted through my curls, found my clit and used the pad of his thumb to spread my slick heat over it.

"Harder," I begged. "More."

He pressed down on the taut nub as if it were a button. I bucked and cried out as sensation ripped through me.

"I could come just from looking at you so shameless like this." His gaze hot, he parted my thighs, positioned between and entered me. His cock glided in smoothly.

"Mmm." My lids lowered.

"Look at me." I forced my eyes open. Propped on his arms, he stared at me. "I love you." He withdrew achingly slowly, and I whimpered flexing inner muscles to try to hold him inside.

"It will always be you for me." He slid his hot cock back inside as maddeningly slowly as he had withdrawn it. Ripples of loose pleasure spread outward when he was as far inside of me as he could go. "Do you believe me?" His voice was as strained as his muscles. He wanted to let go as badly as I did. His skin was misted with perspiration. If my hands had been free, I would've run them all over him.

"Yes. I love you, Lucky. Do that again."

He withdrew and he slid back in only a little faster and a little deeper. The ripples constricted centering where we were joined. I lifted my hips as he sank his cock into me again. We began to move together, but once again he set the pace. The heat intensified. The sensations heightened. Our gratification grew. More in and out glides. More pleasure. My heart raced. Our heavy breaths punctured the humid air. Pleasure spooled around my swollen clit. It spiked each time he slid inside me. And he didn't stop. He thrust and withdrew. He pushed in, and he pulled out. Poised on the edge, I fought to maintain my balance. To delay. I didn't want to let go if he didn't let go with me. Then he found my trapped hands and aligned mine to his. Palms to warm palms first, then every single one of our fingertips touched.

"Open your eyes, Angel."

As soon as my gaze hit his, he stiffened inside me and let go, and I let go with him.

Flying,

Flying,

Flying,

Right over the edge with him.

CHAPTER
fourteen

Cleaned up and recently sated, I could barely keep my eyes open as I lay in the bed waiting for Lucky to finish his second shower. The door popped open and I followed the shadow of his form until he stepped into the slice of illumination from the lamp.

"You tired?" Clad only in a white towel, he propped a hip against the side of the bed he usually slept on in hotel rooms, the side closest to the door so he could protect me in case someone broke in. Yeah, not surprisingly, he was that type of guy.

"I am, but in a good way, you know?"

"Yes, for sure." He stroked his hand through my hair and tucked a stray strand behind my ear. ""My sleep was shit without you."

"Everything's shit without you, Lucky."

"It's the same for me without you, Raven. And for everyone else. They've been bitching incessantly. Even Sky's not herself. No one's happy. No one can focus on the music. With you gone, it's been a complete shambles."

"We work together. All of us."

"We do."

"Well, I'm coming back." I took his hand. "And I don't want you to stress about the security. I know you want to protect me. I trust you to keep me safe. I truly will be more careful. I'll try to avoid dangerous situations where at all possible."

"I saw the video of you riding the bull." He raised a brow. "That was rather dodgy."

Ouch. "Well, I learned my lesson. No more overdoing it with the tequila."

"I don't mean to be a hardass, Raven."

"I know. You're just looking out for me." I lifted my hand. He pressed his palm to mine. "I love you."

"I love you, too."

"We still have a little time till we need to get up. You gonna come to bed?"

"As if you needed to ask."

"Well, good, but you're a little wet." I traced the stream that ran down the center of his chest. "You do know that in America we actually use our towels for more than just covering our nakedness."

"Funny girl." His lips curled. He whipped off the towel. My gaze dropped. I suddenly wasn't tired anymore and neither was he.

'No, Sir," Lucky said into his phone while staring down at the morning rush hour traffic below, the taxis and cars snarled in their usual gridlock. On the call he seemed to be enduring a gridlock of another sort, a stalemate of wills between him and Zenith Productions CEO. "No, Mr. Morris, not one bodyguard for the band. One for each member. One for Sky. And one for Raven." I reached for his hand and squeezed his fingers. He turned to regard me and the flint in his eyes softened. "I understand your position. But you must understand that Raven is a part of this band even if she never steps one foot on the stage." He threw his arm around my shoulder. "She's the one who inspired our number one hit. She looks after me, my mates and my sister. She's the heart and harmony of the band. And she's the missing piece that makes me complete. She stays on the tour. That's just the way it is. I'm giving it to you straight. You provide the security I'm asking for or the tour ends."

"You sure you don't want me to come up with you?" Lucky asked me outside the front entrance to the WMO building.

"No. I can do this. I can take care of myself as long as I know you're there for me."

"That's a given." His handsome face was earnest.

"That's just the way it is," I returned just as earnestly using the phrase he had used with Morris. Standing on the sidewalk, his long legs encased in worn denim, the wind tossed around layers of his jet-black hair. In his aviator shades with his tattooed Dragon peeking at me above his collar, he was doing more than stalling out my momentum to go inside and face Suzanne Smith, he was stopping traffic. All along the sidewalk people on their way into work stutter stepped and turned their heads to look back at him no doubt wondering why he looked so familiar. Beyond the sexiness, they could tell he was somebody special. His charisma was just that strong, and with his music vaulting up the charts it was only a matter of time before he was recognized everywhere.

"You know it." He pulled me closer, framing my face in his hands. I felt his eyes searching mine even though they were hidden behind his shades. "You hit Smith with everything you have and what not. No compromise. Yeah?"

I nodded. "Your puzzle piece is planning to follow your example." I sighed. "But I better get inside. It's getting late. I don't want to start off on the wrong foot."

"Smith can wait a minute." His lips slowly curled. "I need a kiss."

"So do I." I slid my hands up into his satiny hair and lowered my head. He angled one way, and directed by the caress of his thumbs along my jawline, I tilted the other. Desire blazed the instant his mouth touched mine. He brushed his lips over mine, once, twice and on the third pass he deepened the connection giving me a little tongue. I felt it to my core, my knees noticeably weak when he ended the kiss a too-soon moment later.

"Go." I took a step away from him, wobbling a bit without his steadying guide. "Finish what you need to in Jersey. I'll see you later."

I watched him mount the Ducati. Lucky Spencer straddling a red, black and chrome motorcycle and revving the engine was a spectacle not to be missed. I only turned away after he steered it into the traffic. Straightening my shoulders, my steps efficiently brisk, I entered the building, but I stopped short when I saw the two women at the security desk. "What are you guys doing here?"

"Supporting you, silly." Sky skipped over and gave me an enthusiastic hug which I returned just as exuberantly.

"What she said," Marsha stated when I peeled back from Lucky's sister to look at her. "You're the leader of this triad. Where you go we follow. The three amigos." She smiled. I grinned goofily. Apparently, I was not going into my showdown with the exec alone after all.

TOGETHER WE FILED into the same conference room where Marsha and I had signed contracts many months ago. Suzanne Smith sat at the head of the long table. Intelligent dark brown eyes alert and ready to frame his next shot, Ignacio Katzman, the director of Rock Fuck Club was just to the right of her. I moved to take the first seat on the left. My entourage filled the available spots on the same side of the table as me. Not a triad any longer. My group had grown by one. Barbara. The exec frowned at her assistant. Marsha and Sky might not be in any real danger in this meeting, but Barbara was. If she pushed her boss on my behalf, she might pay with her job.

"Raven." Smith rapped on the glossy surface of the table with her black and gold pen. "I really don't know why you felt it necessary to bring reinforcements, but that's neither here nor there. I believe I might have given you the wrong impression somehow. This isn't a negotiation. The contract with Miss West as production assistant has run its course, but yours is still in force. I'm still the boss. You're still the employee. Clause 22.3 states…"

"I don't need contractual details recanted to me," I interrupted and kept on going though her gaze narrowed severely. "You need me for this project to be completed. I'm the linchpin, am I not?"

Her eyes widening ever so slightly, she gave me a curt nod.

"So let's begin. You have my proposal. I outlined my acceptable parameters." I sat back in my chair. I had done my homework. I had spoken. It was her turn. Let her end the awkward silence.

"Very well." She set her pen down and peered at me over her steepled fingers. "We'll start with Rocky Walsh. The viewer sees your desire, but where is Mr. Walsh's response to your submission? And what about after-care? I want more than just a blanket wrapped around your shoulder at the end of his scene."

"I can't negotiate for Rocky." I glanced at Sky. She was staring at her hands, which were twisted tightly together.

"I believe you can."

"Up to a point. Maybe."

"Caressing. Kissing. Physical contact." She pressed.

"Caressing above the waist. The blanket stays on." My stomach clenched knowing even with that concession Lucky wouldn't like it.

"Kissing, ok." Sky sucked in a sharp breath "But nothing on the lips."

"Lips are a nonnegotiable, Miss Winters. This is WMO not Nickelodeon."

"One *fake* kiss on the lips." I gave the exec a firm look. "This is television. It's all about camera angles and making the viewers believe what we want them to believe. We can make it appear authentic." I glanced at Ignacio. "Can't we?"

"Absolutely." He nodded, and the brown curls on his head moved like a tumbling wave.

"I suppose." Suzanne pressed her mouth into a flat line, leaned forward, picked up her pen and crossed through something on the paper in front of her. "On to Alec Harris and the painting scene."

"It stays. We can add to it as I proposed."

"I don't see how his and his partner's orientation is relevant to yours."

"Rock Fuck Club is *my* journey of self-discovery, and part of my journey included witnessing their passion, love and commitment to each other." I turned my head. Sky's eyes met mine. She gave me an encouraging smile. Her support flooded me with relief. I just hoped she didn't withdraw it after I redid the scene with Rocky. I returned my attention to the exec. "What I'm offering you is sexy additional footage."

"It's not going to be sexy if it occurs with you all sitting around with your clothes on." Her brow creased. "Tops off for everyone."

"Yes," I agreed. "Alright."

"Very well."

I let out a relieved breath as she crossed out another item. Only one more remained, but I was afraid I might not get it the way I wanted it.

"Really, Miss Winters." She circled around something on her paper and dropped her pen. "That's too much. It's not edgy programming. It's sappy."

"Rock Fuck Club is supposed to be celebrating my right to decide who, where and when. Lucky Spencer is my choice. My final choice in the RFC. You wanted me to show the viewers why he's the one I chose? That scene and those scripted words will do just that."

She shook her head and turned to Ignacio.

"I'm afraid I have to side with Ms. Smith." He dipped his head to her and then glanced at me, his expression broadcasting apology.

Barbara cleared her throat. "It just needs a contrast."

"Pardon?" The exec swiveled her chair to face her assistant.

"Show the sexy times with a voiceover of Raven talking about Lucky."

"Yes, for sure." Marsha leaned forward. "Remind the viewer of Raven's journey with footage from her encounters with all the other guys." My bestie turned to Ignacio. "Focus on Raven's eyes in all those segments like you did in the documentary *The Little Black Dress.* They're expressive. They're her emotional tell. They will make her point eloquently without a single word having to be spoken."

"Miss Winters. Miss West," Suzanne called, stopping us as we started to file out of the room behind everyone else. "Stay. There are a few minor matters we need to resolve before we proceed with filming tonight."

"Alright, only I need to ask Barbara to do something." I caught the secretary just outside the door. "Could you let Sky wait in your office? Just until we're through?" I asked her.

"Sure. She likes makeup and fashion, right?"

I nodded.

"Good. I have a stack of Vogue magazines at my desk. Only..." She trailed off looking a little unsure.

"Only what?" I queried.

"It's that the other chair in my office is occupied with someone I'm not certain you would want Sky to be alone with." She was purposefully being evasive, but I couldn't figure out why.

"Well, Sky can take care of herself, unless it's an axe murderer in there." I paused, and she shook her head, albeit it seemed to me somewhat reluctantly. "We shouldn't be long."

"Raven, I have another meeting scheduled after this one." The exec tapped her pen on the table top.

"Yes, of course." I turned and pulled out my chair again. Marsha took the one next to it. We exchanged a quick look. We were both confused by Barbara's behavior.

"You negotiated quite capably, Miss Winters."

I set my speculation aside about Barbara to acknowledge the uncharacteristic compliment from the exec. "Thank you." Was it my imagination that she seemed overly eager to move the meeting along?

"You're welcome." She rolled her pen between her hands. "You continue to surprise me." I couldn't tell from those words or her expression whether that was a good or a bad thing. "But never presume to bring uninvited guests to a private meeting with me again. Is that understood?"

Gulp. "Yes."

"Especially not underage ones."

"Sky's not underage. She's five years older than her brother."

The exec's eyes widened slightly.

"Does what you need to discuss involve her?" My tone was terse. Like Lucky I didn't appreciate Sky's differences being highlighted.

"No." She cleared her throat and shuffled her papers. "I have a simple addendum to your first contract that I would like you to sign." She slid a paper toward me entitled: Rock Fuck Club Documentary. I skimmed the details quickly.

"I'm not interested," I told her flatly. WMO wanted me to agree to a series of in depth interviews about the guys I had been with for the Rock Fuck Club, including the one I had been with before I had started it. "I'm not talking about Ivan Carl on camera." Too personal. Too fresh. Too much potential to hurt Marsha and Lucky.

"I have signed authorizations from everyone else involved already."

"Lucky's bandmates agreed?" That was surprising.

"Just so."

I blanched. The Dragons had probably been coerced into it. WMO and Zenith Production seemed to have some sort of behind closed doors alliance. "What about Ryland from Noir?" He was signed with Black Cat Records.

She nodded.

"Ashland Keys?" He had his own label.

"Yes."

My stomach sunk. I found this all a little hard to wrap my head around. What would those two say? I hadn't actually hooked up with them.

"JGB?" My voice squeaked. The controversial rapper had tried to force me.

"He took a little while."

"You dropped all of the charges I filed against him?" I guessed.

She nodded.

"What did you offer the others?" My eyes narrowed.

"An upfront stipend. Free advertising across all of WMO's social media platforms. Residual royalties. The usual enticements."

"Why would you do all that for a series that hasn't even been released yet? For one that needs so much revision? One that's so disappointing?"

"I never said it was a disappointment. In fact, we've never received such favorable scores from beta viewers, our sponsorship slots are completely filled. There's even a waiting list well into a proposed third season. That's why I'm so adamant about re-filming. This could be a monster if we all pull together. We need more content. We need to be ready to capitalize when this takes off. I didn't get where I am today by reacting. I got here by being proactive. "How many emails do you receive each day about the Rock Fuck Club?"

"Two, sometimes three hundred."

"WMO is getting thousands."

"But how?"

"Our contact information is first in the Google analytics. After all, we own the concept of the RFC."

"You don't own me." I lifted my chin.

"Correct. And that's why we're here, right now behind closed doors." She picked up her pen. Scribbled something on a pad of notebook paper and lifted it to show me.

"A million dollars?" Holy fucking shit.

"Per episode. As they air. With royalties direct to you ten years out. If you sign that addendum. If you agree to the interviews."

"You've given me a lot to think about. I'll have to get back to you." I remembered what I had read about negotiation tactics. A miracle that I could remember anything the way my brain was spinning on that amount.

"I'm sorry. I'll need an answer now. Showtime. A&E.   Our competitors are already scrambling to copy what we've done. You sign now, or the offer is withdrawn...along with the opportunity for Marsha to direct the documentary."

The million dollars I didn't really care about. I knew too well that wealth didn't equal happiness. Being included and supported in loving relationships trumped any financial windfalls.

But directing? That was my best friend's dream served up on a silver WMO emblazoned platter.

How could I say no to that?

CHAPTER fifteen

"**L**ET'S DISPENSE WITH THE FORMALITY. I'm sure you get that I don't like you." I didn't trust her. The bottom line was her sole motivation. That she would make a deal with a guy like JGB was eye opening and frankly a bit disturbing. "And you don't particularly care for me. But just call me Raven, and I'll call you Suzanne. Are you ok with that?"

She nodded. "Would you like me to write that down...Raven?"

I shook my head. Being on a first name basis leveled the playing field. Now I brought out the bigger guns. "I want the Rock Fuck Club title and the concept returned to me if WMO takes the series in a direction that I don't approve of."

"No. Absolutely not."

"That's a nonstarter Suzanne. If you don't have the authority to make that concession find me someone who does."

"I have all the final say on every aspect of this project." The force of her quietly spoken statement practically rattled the steel girders of the building.

"Good. Then you understand why I insist. I started RFC. It represents me. It ultimately reflects on me. But it reflects Marsha and every other twenty something woman in the world we live in today. A confusing world where we are told to aspire to be perfect princesses in towers from the time we're young, then are bombarded constantly by contradictory messages in the media. Ones that tell us that our worth is largely dependent on how sexy we are or whether or not we secure the attention of a man. Yet, if we attempt to explore our sexuality or define it outside socially accepted parameters we're given derogatory labels. Slut, whore, and the like."

"I agree with all of that."

"Then make those sentiments part of the mission statement, and we won't have any problems with creative differences."

"As to the theme…"Suzanne began, but I wasn't finished.

"As far as the background stuff. The additional filming. I'll confess it makes me tired to even consider getting back in front of the camera, but I can see the value of it. If another woman can learn from my mistakes and maybe take a less circuitous route to the right guy like Lucky then that's a good thing."

I turned to Marsha. "Are you ok with what she wants you to do? You'll have to spend a lot of time with me. A lot of time on the road. No more Texas. No more chats at Joey's. We likely won't see our families very much, not for a long time."

"I'm ok, Raven. I'm sitting beside the closest family member I have."

My eyes immediately filled. I felt the same way about her. I managed a nod.

"So," I turned back to the exec. "There's a couple of minor things left to quibble about if I say yes. I'd like WMO to provide security for me. If this thing blows up as big as you think it will then I want to be protected. Mr. Morris has agreed to provide a bodyguard for me while I'm on the tour, but I would like WMO to take on that expense when I'm not. And I also need help with the day to day correspondence and PR stuff that goes along with RFC. If Barbara is available to travel..."

"She is," Suzanne interrupted, her hazel eyes gleaming. "It would be a perfect match. You seem to have developed a rapport with her, and she's been chafing to get more involved with the series. But at this juncture, I would also like to settle the matter of the second season while I have you both here." She turned her bottom-line-motivated gaze to my bestie. "Miss West, WMO would like you to star in Rock Fuck Club season two."

"I don't know." My bestie's baby blues grew wide.

"Come, come, Miss West. You know what to expect. You support the cause. Raven just said that RFC represents you as well. You'll continue to be paired together. The contractual particulars can be hashed out at another time. I'm only asking for a verbal commitment today."

"But the documentary."

"Season two and the documentary will be filmed concurrently. Mr. Katzman will direct season two. You will direct the documentary about Raven with his guidance. We'll keep the production crew together from season one for both projects."

"That makes sense, I guess." Marsha glanced at me.

"Only do it if you want to, Mars." I reached for her hand. "You can do the documentary and not the other. Why don't we both take a couple of days to think about everything?"

"I can't let either of you leave this room before I have a commitment." Suzanne shook her head. "Too much is at stake here."

"I'll do it." Marsha's voice was steady. "Season Two and the Documentary. I've got nothing to lose, and a lot of money and experience to gain." Her eyes were no longer wide. They sparkled with anticipation as she regarded the exec. "Best get prepared for another tough round of negotiations. I have my own ideas and my own personality. You'll have to make adjustments to accommodate them."

"I look forward to it." Suzanne nodded to Marsha and tapped my contract with her pen. I stared at the empty line and the x by it that awaited my signature.

"I'll have to run this by Lucky first."

Suzanne frowned.

"I can call him right now. With you here in the room."

"Agreed."

I took my cell out of my cross body bag. I had turned the ringer off before the meeting, but the display was alight with multiple missed texts from the Dragons' frontman.

Missed call from Lucky Spencer.

Lucky: Is Sky with you?

Lucky: Never mind. Rocky told me she is

Lucky: Sky just called me. What's going on with you and Smith?

Lucky: Just got out of my meeting with Morris. He worked out a deal with Black Cat. Once we finish our remaining dates...The Dragons are the opening band for Noir!!! Huge stadium shows. Even Wembley. The bad news is he worked out a not so hot deal with your boss at WMO. Call me. We need to talk.

Lucky: ---?

Lucky: ---?

I dialed his number.

"Angel." He answered on the first ring. I could hear heavy bass thumping in the background. Sound check already? That meant it was already lunchtime. My stomach grumbled. "How'd your meeting go?"

"I'm still in it." My golden eyes clashed with Suzanne's hazel green ones.

"Those wankers want you to do even more than before, don't they?"

"Yes. But I ironed out a lot of stipulations. Creative control. Security. Secretarial support."

"Impressive."

"Yeah." I guessed it was. I sat up straighter. Praise from him made me feel like I was light enough to float in a wide open sky the color of his eyes.

"She's listening isn't she?"

"Absolutely."

"I didn't really have much of a choice on my end. Morris has me and my mates by the balls."

"Yes."

"She has a tight leash on you, too?"

"Yes. But I can snap it if I need to." At least I hoped I could. "I started the RFC with good intentions like you're always reminding me. I'm planning to continue the concept the best I can. Marsha has agreed to do season two, and she's directing the backstory interviews. RFC. WMO. They're not going away. I'm playing my part. But from now on I play it by *my* rules. And that means checking with my boyfriend first. Are you ok with that?"

"I love you, Raven Elizabeth Winters."

"I love you, too."

"Do whatever you need to do. You can take care of yourself, and I trust you to do right by us. Cheers and what not, Angel. You have my full support."

CHAPTER
sixteen

"THIS IS MY FAVORITE VIEW IN the whole world." I stared deeply into the fathomless blue of Lucky's eyes, sliding the pad of my thumb along the bottom of the right one and then the left to smudge the kohl lines I had drawn beneath them.

"I'm quite fond of the one in front of me as well." His gaze as smoky as the eye makeup he now wore thanks to me, Lucky's long slender fingers flexed on my hips, a skin to skin connection that crackled.

Outside our private world of two, the usual flurry of preshow dressing room activity was cranked up to a near frenzy. Everyone was coasting high on the Noir news, and maybe we were all a little more wound up about the additional WMO filming that would follow the Dragons' performance later tonight. The opening band was already on stage, directly behind the dressing room wall. Their music vibrated the sheetrock as Alec paced back and forth in the small twelve by twelve foot space. Lucky's best friend was dressed in jeans and a button down shirt, every wisp of his hair styled just so. His Fender was already strapped on. His shooting star makeup streaked across his face, and his jade green eyes were amped up and glittery with nervous energy. Meanwhile, wearing a white tee paired with one of his partner's button downs and jeans, Cody chilled on a folding chair, his ankles crossed and his booted feet propped up on the vibrating wall. He was so absorbed in a game on his phone that I don't think he even noticed Sky as she patiently applied his assortment of treble clef tears. Lucky's sister looked lovely in a short floral frock with long bell-like sleeves. Hovering nearby in jeans and a black vest sans shirt was Rocky. With his sticks, he drummed a ratt-tatt-tatt on the counter beside her makeup kit as he waited for his turn with Sky. She pretended not to notice him or his reflection in the mirror while he did the same.

"Only fond?" I skimmed my hand down the center of Lucky's bare chest, reveling in the way his eyes darkened to sapphire in response to my caress.

"Maybe a tiny bit more than fond." He gave me his cocky half-smile.

"Nothing tiny about any part of you." I ran my hand lower, tiptoed my fingers over the zipper of his jeans and across his hard length. His breath hitched. I leaned in for a kiss. His lips were an irresistible feast. His kiss even more so as he took over, plunging his wet and very wicked tongue into my mouth. He ended it way too soon. Capturing my hands, he removed them from the prize of his cock and pointed with his chin to a spot over my shoulder where Ignacio and the rest of his crew were filming us.

"Sorry. I forgot." Bright light blazed from Ernie College's tripod. A mic hung from Les Turner's sound boom. Ignacio Katzman balanced his video camera on his shoulder while Carla Middleton hovered to the side with a fluffy makeup brush at the ready.

"I want you." Lucky exhaled. "Very badly. But I've got a show to put on first and then..."

Then we had all those extra scenes to film. Rocky, a kiss and aftercare. Alec and Cody. Then us. Lucky dipped his finger inside the low slung waistband of my jeans. "I like these." His voice was husky.

"I like the way you like them." My lips lifted. I enjoyed his method of centering my focus on him. "Carla bought them and a whole bunch of other stuff for me." I waved at the statuesque black woman who had made me look almost as beautiful as she did tonight. Marsha was standing beside her, dressed to kill as usual. Her mustard yellow crochet frock had flowing bell sleeves like Sky's, but that was where the similarity between them ended. My bestie's dress was shorter. It showed her lightly tanned skin between the stitching and lots of cleavage through the front laces that crisscrossed down the center of her chest. Her brow was creased. She had her GoPro out. She had already started on the documentary and was recording the film crew filming us.

"What do you think of the rest of my outfit?" I pulled away from Lucky to do a little fashion spin. I had knotted a one-size-too-small dragon emblazoned 'Get Lucky' tee below my breasts with the jeans he seemed to appreciate and sandals that had lots of silver buckles and black straps.

"The clothes are almost sexy enough to be worthy of you." He brushed a long length of my hair from the front to the back and dipped his head to brush a soft kiss beneath my ear. Tingles erupted on my skin as he breathed into it. "I'm doing you with just those high heels on later, you know."

"Promise?" I tilted my head to give him a look through my lowered lashes.

"Nothing's going to stop me."

I smiled. I knew he meant more, that not even WMO or Suzanne Smith's agenda were going to come between us again.

"Later." He stroked the back of his knuckles down my cheek. His silver rings flashed reflecting the dressing mirror lights as he moved to the center of the room. "Ok, Dragons," he announced, cleared his throat and ran through a quick low to high scale and back again before circling his hand up in the air. "Let's breathe some fire."

"I'm not finished with Rocky yet." Sky complained.

"You would spend hours on him if I allowed it, dearest. Leave well enough alone." He raised a brow, and she blushed. Rocky stood, grabbed his vest from the back of the chair and put it back on before he brushed a kiss on Sky's notably rosy cheek. Her blush deepening, she followed him with her eyes and her body as he joined her brother. Alec stepped closer while adjusting his strap to sling his bass to his back. Cody ducked near him, and the guys formed a tight huddle. This was something they did before every performance. I couldn't hear what Lucky said to them inside the circle this time, but whatever it was the guys came out of it smiling.

Catching my eyes on him, Lucky gave me a nod, then turned to exit the room. The guys followed their leader. The small space suddenly seemed inexplicably smaller minus all the Dragons inside it.

"You wanna stay and pine after him or go see him put on his show?" Marsha asked. Documentary director. Soon to be star of season two. Yet, still my bestie, looking out for me and giving me the business at the same time.

"You know the answer to that one, Mars."

"Do you think Rocky's makeup came out alright?" Sky looked fretful as she moved closer to us.

"I didn't notice his makeup," Marsha said. "Too busy scoping out the sculpted rest of him like you were."

Sky nodded in agreement, not bothering to deny it. "Once I start touching him I can't focus."

"The hammers are great, Sky." I told her. "You always do a fantastic job."

"You did too with my brother." She smiled her approval. We heard stomping feet and cheers from the other side of the wall. It was almost time for the Dragons.

"Ok, girls. Where we gonna watch from?" Marsha queried. "Side stage or balcony?"

"Side stage," I answered. "I like to see Lucky and his fans as he connects with them."

"I have to work the merch booth." Sky grumbled.

"Get one of the roadies to do it," I suggested.

"No. That's alright." The bright light in Sky's blue eyes dimmed. "I've seen Rocky...I mean, the guys many times. And the girls will be hanging all over him." She sighed. "It's better to keep my distance."

"Sky, maybe you and he..."

"No, Raven." She gave me a sad smile. "I'm chuffed for you and my brother. Truly, I am. But it's best for me," she swallowed, "if I don't get my hopes up, for, you know..."

"Ok. But here." I wrapped my arms around her and Marsha embraced both of us. "The guys aren't the only ones who can do a group huddle."

After we broke Sky seemed a little less sad. She went one direction out in the hall and Marsha and I turned and went the other, linking our arms together until we reached the stage. The lights were off. Up on his riser, Rocky was a tall shadow behind his drums. Alec stood with his bass to the left of the center mic and Cody with his Les Paul was on the far right.

"Ladies and gentlemen." Lucky's dramatic disembodied voice

over the sound system gave me chills. "The time is here. Come take my hand. Strike up the band and start the show." Cody played a scintillating power chord. The overhead lights blasted on. Rocky clacked the energetic count on his sticks. Alec climbed up on the drummer's riser and jumped off. The three floor pyramids pulsed cool neon colored patterns and then Lucky strutted onto the stage from the opposite side from us wearing an undone silver sequin jacket with no shirt on beneath it. He clapped his hands over his head, and the crowd went completely nuts. They screamed even louder when he reached the center mic and started singing. Even I swooned inwardly, though I had seen him command an audience like this many times before. Lucky and the Dragons were almost too much for a club to contain. They were going to totally rock the stadium scene.

After the first song Lucky ditched the jacket. A girl close to the stage caught it, brought it to her chest and practically passed out. I knew the game. He had just made her and all the friends she had with her fans for life. But even though I understood it, I still felt a little twinge of jealousy.

By the time the encore arrived, Lucky's black hair was plastered to his skull, and his jeans were soaked as if he had been in a downpour. He exited the stage on my side, his eyes glowing brighter than his glittery slashes, and he shook his perspiration soaked head at me. I squealed, and he kissed me, long and hard and deep. The twinge of irrational jealousy completely forgotten, I jumped up and wrapped my legs around his waist, and he walked us backward into the closest wall. He practically had my shirt off when Alec tapped on his shoulder so hard it vibrated through his body into mine.

"Put it away until later, mate. We gotta get back out there. The crowd's not done with us. They're demanding another encore."

"Ok. Alright. But I'm not going alone." Lucky took my hand, headed toward the stage, pulling me along with him.

"No." I skip-walked as I dragged my feet. He had never taken me out onto the stage before. As his girlfriend, I wasn't certain I would be welcome, and deep down maybe I was a little afraid of his female fans. After all they had practically trampled me once already.

"I insist," he said and tucked me close to his right side. The stomping and clapping ended abruptly as soon as the crowd saw us. A guitar tech approached. He handed Lucky his acoustic guitar. Cody moved to the lead singer's left. He had an acoustic of his own. I stared out at the sea of faces in a bit of a daze as Lucky put his hands on my shoulders and moved me into the center of a spotlight. He curled his ringed fingers around the mic. "I'd like to introduce you to Raven Winters. My girl. 'She's the One'." The crowd hushed. An anticipatory rush opened my heart and then Lucky filled it as he strummed the sweet eloquent song he had written for me while Cody played countermelody. Tears pricked my eyes. It was one thing to hear the song played from a position in the audience or on the side stage. It was quite another to be standing in the spotlight with him singing it directly to me.

If I hadn't already been totally and completely his, this gesture would have wrapped it up and tied it tight with a perfect bow. Joy streamed unchecked from my eyes when the song was over. Hands to my chest as if to hold the memory to my heart, I watched Lucky and Cody take their bows.

"I love you," I told him, stopping and turning to face him once we were off the stage. "Thank you."

He waved his rhythm guitarist on to the meet and greet and pressed me into a darkened alcove. "Don't thank me for loving you."

"I'm not." Going up on my tiptoes, I brought my mouth to his, kissing him tenderly. "I'm thanking you for that. For what you did out there. For not just telling me you love me but showing me and the entire world and for giving me a memory I will always cherish."

"Ah Raven." He set his forehead to mine. "I want to hate the RFC and all the craziness that comes with it. But how can I when it brought you to me?"

"Then we won't hate it. We'll keep moving forward together, and we'll reshape the craziness into a unique and beautiful reality that works for the two of us."

CHAPTER
seventeen

O N MY WAY TO THE MERCH BOOTH to help Sky, I wandered around the periphery of the meet and greet room watching the guys joke and laugh with their fans. Tonight, there wasn't any Lucky juice in the frontman's hands. He had his shirt on. He had listened to me. He had paid attention. All my concerns couldn't be alleviated, but he made concessions for me, and I loved him for it.

A trip down the long corridor, across the stage and through the empty concert hall strewn with empty plastic cups brought me to the mezzanine. Behind the table, Sky was swamped with customers, but she handled it with her usual aplomb. She trained her bright customer-first smile on me when she saw me. I scooted behind the table with her and we fell into an easy, practiced pattern taking turns with the iPad swiping credit cards. We ran out of merchandise long before we ran out of customers.

Apologizing profusely, I fielded a few grumbles from my side of the table, but Sky made a joke of it and all the patrons on her side were smiling as they left. Most of them anyway. Two guys remained. Good looking ones, a brunette and a blond, built like personal trainers. The brunette leaned in, brushed Sky's long hair aside and she giggled at whatever he whispered into her ear. That was the last thing he did before being unceremoniously lifted into the air and body slammed against an adjacent wall by a big angry Welshman.

"Did he have permission to touch you, Sky?" Rocky asked, without removing his hold or his incensed gaze from the man he apparently perceived as a threat.

"Put him down, Rocky." Looking mortified, she stamped her hands on her hips. "He was only asking me to have a drink with him and his friend."

"Dude." The guy shrugged out of the drummer's now lax hold. "Is she your sister, your girlfriend or what?" He straightened his shirt, and his friend came to stand beside him.

"Neither, not that it's any of your business," Rocky answered the question, but shifted his attention to Sky. "You're not going anywhere with them." His mahogany brows were an implacable v over his golden eyes.

"You need to get a grip," the blond told the drummer before turning back to Sky. "What do you say, Sweetness? There's a bar with a view of the water a couple of blocks from here. They have good burgers, and decent drinks. Come check it out with us."

"I don't know." Sky looked conflicted. She twisted her hands. Tension buzzed in the air. Two against one, but I wouldn't bet against the drummer.

"Bring your friend." The brunette gestured to me. "It'll be a double date."

"Raven has a boyfriend. She's..."

"Not going anywhere with either of you." Rocky cursed under his breath and moved, grabbing Sky by her upper arm. "She's underage, lads." Sky gaped at him and his lie. "Now move along. Both of you. Before I call security."

The guys took off fast. Like back home when you get a midnight craving for a Whataburger with jalapeños.

"That isn't true, Rocky." Sky's delicate brow creased. "Why did you lie?"

"Why were you flirting with two guys you don't even know?" He frowned. "And who gave you that dress? With you bent over the table, they could see your tits." He whipped off his 'Get Hammered' tee. "No wonder they wanted to take you out." He put his shirt over her head, threading her arms into the sleeves while she stared at him with a hurt expression.

"I wasn't flirting. I was just being myself. They were nice. They said I looked pretty." She blinked her wide blue eyes at him. "I like this dress. Carla gave it to me. And you flirt with plenty of girls you don't even know." She backed away from him, took off his shirt and threw it at him. Rocky looked stunned as it landed on the carpet at his feet.

"Are you totally clueless?" I told him as he stood still as a statue staring at Sky as she stormed away. "You had no right to interfere, and you insulted her no less."

"What the bloody hell do you expect me to do, Raven?" He turned his head slightly to regard me. His jaw was clamped tight. "Let her go off with two strangers?" he spit out. "Let her get raped or worse? She's like a child..."

"She's not."

"She is," he insisted. "A beautiful one with a body that makes a man weak and eyes that make him dream about impossible things..." He trailed off, giving me a sharp look as if I had somehow coerced those truths from him. "Bullocks," he said. "Forget I said that last part." He sounded resigned. "Lucky sent me to fetch you. The meet and greet is over. They've got the cameras set up in the motor coach." He shook his head. "Let's get this thing done. It'll be the icing on a shit cake. Might as well have Sky and her brother mad at me all at once."

"LEAN IN. MORE," Ignacio instructed from his position on the opposite couch, and Rocky brought his face closer to mine. "No. Stop. Cut," the director said, and the rest of the crew grumbled. "Let's take a break everyone."

I slid off of Rocky's lap, immediately cold in just my lacy bra and panties without all his warmth. He didn't seem to feel the chill even though he was only in jeans. He stood and stretched. The director set his camera aside, moving straight to the kitchenette and the Keurig for more coffee, along with the rest of the crew. It was late. We had been at this for over an hour. Lucky and the others lounged in the back of the bus waiting their turn to film so we could call it a night. But we were nowhere close to that yet.

The tenderness part of the redo Rocky had worked brilliantly. I had seen the playback. Everyone was happy with how it had turned out. But the kiss. It was obvious Rocky wanted no part of it, even if we weren't planning to have our lips touch.

"Hey." I tapped his arm softly. His bicep was rock-hard tense. "What can I do to make this better?"

"Nothing, Raven. I'm sorry." His unfocused gold eyes blinked a couple of times before they cleared. "Well, perhaps if you could rewind time, take back the words I said to Sky and help me not be such an arse to her, that would be a fine place to start."

"She still not talking to you?"

"I've called and texted her a dozen times. No response. She's frozen me out."

I winced. Lucky's sister's way of handling anger was to pretend the person she was mad at didn't exist. I had seen her keep it up for an entire week with Cody after he had rearranged her makeup chest as a joke. "Did you tell her you're sorry?"

"Yes." He shrugged one shoulder. "But I think I'm going to need to do more. In person. Get her alone. Only, I don't want to do it in front of Lucky. He'd be steaming-mad if he found out how I behaved."

I nodded commiseratively. He was right. I suddenly got an idea. "Listen. Let's get this fake kiss over with. Then while Lucky and the rest of us are busy you can go find Sky and make it right?"

"Yeah, that would be good." He nodded, and his expression lightened. "You need to loosen up for this too, you know. You're stiff as a board."

"Me?" I put a hand on my hip and arched a brow. "You're the one who sighs every time we get close."

"True. What if you pretend I'm him?" His mischievous grin appeared. "I'm sexier of course, but you can use your imagination."

"Ok. I'll give that a try. And you can pretend I'm Sky."

"Raven." He glanced around checking to see if anyone might have heard.

"We all know how it is, Rocky. Admit it. You were jealous tonight. That's why you acted the way you did."

"I won't...I would never..." He sighed heavily.

"I know. I get it." His reservations. Hers. But was being a couple really as impossible as they each seemed to believe?

I WATCHED THE playback on Ignacio's camera with Rocky's stubble scruffy chin scratchy on the bare skin of my neck as he looked over my shoulder. I swiveled around to face him when we both had seen it.

"It's great."

"Isn't it?" He gave me a wry grin while the rest of the WMO crew moved to the bunk area to get their equipment ready for the next scene. "Lucky's going to hate it."

"I'll remind him that I was pretending you were him." Which was the truth. And if the intense way Rocky had been looking at me when he had slowly brought his mouth toward mine was indicative of his feelings for Sky he was showing incredible restraint not to act on them.

"Tell me what?" Lucky asked, sidestepping the light tripod that blocked the center aisle.

"It's done," I informed him breathily. He wore only jeans. He had his shirt off like the rest of the guys in the band. It was what Smith wanted. Lots of skin. And of course, looking at him, seeing his half-naked body and chiseled chest made my pulse race.

"Finally." Lucky shot Rocky a dark look.

"Relax, mate." The drummer waved his hands in front of his body. "I didn't truly kiss her. Groped her instead." He backed away. "Your woman has such a fine ass and…" He trailed off as Sky suddenly appeared on the opposite end of the lounge. Her gaze clashed with his for a long uncomfortable moment before she turned completely back around, murmuring under her breath about taking a taxi to the hotel with Marsha.

"Sky, wait." Moving quickly, Rocky caught her as she tried to descend the stairs.

"Let go of me." She glanced down at his hand on her wrist then up at him.

"I want to apologize."

"No need. You're free to do as you like." She shrugged out of his hold.

"Will I see you later?" he asked her retreating form. He didn't get an answer. But if the angry slap of a hand against the bus door was any indication, he might want to plan on steering clear of her in the short term.

"You done with your part, Raven?" Alec asked, righting the tripod after he bumped it. His partner ducked past it. Lucky was glaring at Rocky.

"Yes, we're done," I answered Alec.

"What's that all about, then?" Lucky asked, moving toward his drummer.

"Nothing that concerns you," Rocky snarled at him in reply and headed toward the stairs.

"What the bloody hell?" Brows raised, Alec cast a questioning glance around at everyone else.

"Don't ask." I shook my head and touched Lucky's shoulder softly to draw his attention to me. "Give the two of them some space. They'll work it out." At least I hoped they would.

"Ok, all," Ignacio announced and tossed the Styrofoam cup he had been drinking from into the sink. It was his third cup, but his hands were steady as he reached for the camera he had briefly set aside. "There's enough drama on this bus to fill the entire second season of RFC. But let's get the current one squared away first, shall we?"

"Yes," I agreed quickly.

"Sure," Alec said.

"Whatever you need, mate." Cody bobbed his head and his sandy brown curls bounced. "I'm game."

"Good." Ignacio pointed over his shoulder. "We'll start in the aisle between the bunks with just Raven and Alec. Bring Cody in next. Then Lucky. We'll see how it goes from there."

"Got it." Lucky put his hands on my shoulders and turned me to face him. "I know why you proposed doing the scene this way," he said low as the crew and everyone else moved toward the back. "Alec and Cody are certainly appreciative."

"I hope it works."

"You're giving them a platform to stick it to the marketing team at Zenith for opposing their relationship. It'll be brilliant." Before I could say more, he lowered his head and pressed a sweet kiss to my lips. I accepted it, wanting more of course. I was always greedy when it came to him.

"Excuse me," Carla said, and we broke apart. "Let me touch up your makeup. Your face is a little shiny." She had her powder brush in her hand.

"I'll see you in just a bit." Lucky told me, squeezing my shoulders before he scooted past us. He wasn't scheduled to appear until later in the scene.

"You look great." Carla smiled at me after she brushed on a couple of coats. I thanked her and moved to stand closer to Alec. He was waiting for me at the entrance to the bunk area.

"You ready?" he asked me, his jade eyes assessing me.

"Yeah. How about you?"

"I'm good. But it's been a while since I undressed a woman." He sucked his lips taut over his teeth, something I knew he only did when he was nervous.

"You'll do fine. Try pretending I'm Cody." I grabbed his hand and squeezed it. His skin was ice cold. "It'll be alright. Truly." I tugged him out of the front lounge and into the scene. We had to slide in side by side past the equipment and the crew to take our place in the aisle between the bunks. "We're friends. Family." I turned around to give him my back, drawing my hair to the front so he could have easier access. "Just start with the clasp between my shoulders. Do whatever feels natural. We'll go from there."

"If you say so. I probably need to warm my hands." He placed them on my shoulders. He stroked his thumbs back and forth over my skin. He was gentle. It felt nice to be touched by him and even nicer when he lowered his head and pressed a firm kiss into the side of my neck. "Your skin's so soft," he mumbled, his breath tickling my skin. "And you smell good. Different than Cody. "He slid his fingers down the center of my back following my spine. He stopped when he reached my bra strap. I tipped my head so I could see him over my shoulder. Our eyes met.

"Different is good," I said. "If we were all the same life would be a boring. You're very handsome Alec." His lips spread into a slow grin from my praise.

And that was when I think we both realized that Ignacio had already started filming us.

"Thank you." Alec deftly unhooked my bra. "I'd like to see more of you. Would you show me?"

"Yes." I spun around to face him, holding the scraps of lace in place over my breasts. His gaze dipped then lifted. "You're gorgeous, Raven." He reached out and gently removed my hands so he could slide the straps down my arms. Then, he tossed the bra aside. Brushing my hair to the back again, he studied me for a moment tracing my curves with his eyes before he traced me softly with his hands. Not a sexual exploration. I could feel the difference, but it was sensual. Awareness of him as a man and me as a woman, it was definitely there. My breasts grew heavy and my nipples hardened as he continued to touch me.

"I see you." He skimmed his hands down my ribs. "My body reacts to you. You are undeniably attractive. But I want Cody. His smooth skin. His scent. His tongue."

"I see you, too." I reached for Alec, framed his face and swept my thumb over his lips. He parted them for me. I hissed. He had flicked his tongue out to lick me. I came up on my toes. Unscripted, unplanned, I kissed him full on his lips. They were warm and firm, but they weren't lush. "You're the vixen," I realized. "I always thought it was Cody."

Suddenly another set of male hands slid around my waist from behind. A firm kiss to my neck, a subtle musky masculine scent, and a smile from Alec that wasn't directed at me.

"Hello, love," the rhythm man told his partner, and Cody and Alec kissed each other with me sandwiched in the middle between them. It was a deep kiss. A long one. Their groans vibrated through their masculine chests to me, and even though they both wore jeans I could feel their cocks lengthen on either side of me, hardness in front and behind. But being with them wasn't anything like the *ménage a trois* with the rap duo. This was deeper. This was love, love that Alec and Cody had for each other and love that the three of us had as a family. They separated. They took each other's hands leaving an opening that Lucky slipped through before they closed the circle. Now I wasn't alone in the middle anymore.

"Hello, Angel." The frontman glided his hands along my hips, his thumbs dipping into the edge of my panties. My breath caught, my skin electrified from his touch. Nipples tight, clit throbbing, I instantly ached for more.

"You three are hot as hell to watch," Lucky whispered. He stared down at me, his gaze possessive. "But it's time to kiss your favorite Dragon. Your only Dragon."

CHAPTER
eighteen

WE ONLY HAD TO DO A COUPLE OF additional takes with the four of us. Basically only close-ups to complement what we had already done.

"It's awesome," I told Ignacio after we reviewed the tape.

"I agree." Lucky stood behind me, his hands on my shoulders again. I had my bra back on, but other than that I hadn't bothered with additional clothing. I wasn't self-conscious in only my lingerie. Ignacio and the film crew had seen me in various stages of undress. So for that matter had Alec and Cody after being on the bus with me.

"I hope Smith signs off on all of it." I gnawed on my lip.

"She already gave the thumbs up on the segment we redid with Rocky," Ignacio informed me. "So are you ready for the last part with Lucky? Or should we postpone it until the morning?"

"Sorry to interrupt." Alec leaned in and kissed my cheek. "We're gonna take off." The rhythm man smiled at me from his spot beside the bassist. "Cody and I fancy some alone time."

"Alright. See you later." I returned Cody's smile and watched the couple as they walked away holding hands.

"So, what will it be?" Ignacio drew my attention back to him. Above his camera lens, he lifted an inquiring brow.

"We'll continue," Lucky confirmed, then turned to me. "You mentioned something about those heels, Angel. And my fucking you in them. Are you ready to deliver?"

"C1 through C5." I put my hand on his chest and lowered my voice to the sultry tone I knew he liked. "We'll start at the driver's seat and work our way back to the stabbin' cabin. If you can keep up with me," I batted my lashes at him, "I just might end up keeping you." I played the part as if he and I were back in the past. Though we both knew, I had started falling for him from the moment I had landed at his feet.

That line of mine was scripted. It was Ignacio's cue. His camera zoomed in for a closeup. Les dropped the mic closer. Ernie adjusted his light. It was surreal, but this was my life, and it was a great one with Lucky Spencer in it.

"You wrote me a song. I don't have talent with words like you do, but I want you to know what you mean to me. I fell at your feet the first time we met and my heart started falling then, too. You're understanding, protective, smart, talented as hell and far too good for me. I'm sorry it took me longer than it should have to learn to trust again. Thank you for being patient with me while I figured everything out."

"Angel." He stepped closer to me, taking my hands, bringing them to his chest, his eyes blazing bright. "We're on a journey together, and you're the light for me on that path. I'd be lost, alone and in the dark if it weren't for you." His hands slid to my ass. He drew my body more firmly into his. "I love you, Raven."

"I love you, Lucky, and I'm ready right now to take our next step on the path, the one that starts the new beginning of us."

My man suddenly grabbed me. He picked me up and threw me over his shoulder. I gasped as he slapped my ass. My pussy quivered. The pulses in my clit matched the rhythm of his strides as he carried me to the front of the bus.

I hadn't bothered scripting his parts. I had just written in: 'Lucky being sexy.'

And he was.

He always was.

"I HAVEN'T SEEN you since the concert last night. What have you been up to?" I asked Marsha the following evening as she stepped over the VIP rope and dropped down on the big velvety purple sectional beside me.

"Slept late. Hit the gym. The usual hookup. The usual disappointment." She dropped her gaze, but even in the pulsing club lights I could see the shadows in her blue eyes.

"Oh, Mars." I set down my drink on the glass table in front of me, sat beside her and took her hands. "Maybe if you tried a little harder to let Hawk go, you'd find someone worthy of your time."

"Did that work for you after you broke up with Lucky that time?"

"Not, hardly." I shook my head.

"One of a kind guys are impossible to get over." She shrugged a shoulder. A gesture meant to be nonchalant, but there was nothing casual about the way she had felt about my brother. "Can we talk about something else? Like strategy going forward for the behind the scenes interviews?"

"Sure." I let her redirect the conversation. "I love you, Mars."

"I love you, too." She patted my hand and settled back into the couch. "Where's Sky?"

"She and Rocky had a fight last night. I guess she didn't feel like coming out tonight to celebrate."

"And Lucky?"

I lifted my chin. She turned to follow the direction of my gaze. Lucky and the guys had gone to the bar to get champagne. They had ended up surrounded by fans seeking autographs.

"How'd the final scenes turn out?"

"They went pretty well."

"In other words, super-hot."

I nodded. C1 through C5. He had delivered in every way.

"He's a keeper. I'm glad you found him."

"I'm glad he found me."

"Holy shit!" Marsha stood suddenly. I stood, too. She grabbed my arm. I turned to follow her gaze. My eyes widened. It was Sky. She had come after all. Only she wasn't alone. She was with Ivan.

To be continued in Rock F*ck Club #3

For a release alert, follow me on
Bookbub: *https://www.bookbub.com/authors/michelle-mankin*

For teasers, cover and excerpt reveals AND a chance to win an autographed book and swag each month subscribe to my bimonthly

Black Cat Records Newsletter: *http://eepurl.com/Lvgzf*

Made in the USA
Coppell, TX
05 October 2023

22456313R00090